Journey

Lorenzo Lago

Journey by Lorenzo Lago

Copyright 2013, 2026

Correspondence: www.lorenzolago.com

Cover Art: *Tropical Hideaway* by Ken Auster, www.kenauster.com

ISBN# 978-0-615-73529-0

Journey

This book is dedicated to my children, Ryan and Inai. I cherish that our souls are connected for this Earth journey. I honor that I can be 'Dad' to two elegant and engaging souls. I am so grateful, the Universe has been generous to me.

Forever love, Dad

TEARS OF JOY

My computer is the only instrument of technology I brought from the States. Writing with pen and paper is soulful, and good for middle-of-the-night ideas, but my laptop is exceptionally proficient in maintaining the extended comprehension of my final goal. So, I haven't gone totally pure. This may defeat some of the reason for my escaping to this lost peninsula, but who cares! I have no misconception that I am a 21st century man imagining he is part of a Swiss Family Robinson fantasy. Adventure is the key for inspiration, and I also love my comfort zone.

When I feel I need to check my emails, I take a small hike. The closest Internet café (not really an Internet café, more of a lunch counter with two ancient Macs in a back room) is about two miles away from my cottage. I can plug my laptop in here, and the connection with the rest of the world is fairly fast.

Today, I received an email from the wife of an old friend. She writes that her husband was recently diagnosed with cancer, and after a short battle with the disease, he quickly passed away. The cancer was deep inside his body and no treatment could help this late stage of the illness. He didn't have a chance. His wife was letting friends know of his passing. He died in his wife's arms with his children by his side.

It is difficult to read an email like this. It's like passing an automobile accident and seeing the despair of all who are involved. Your heart just bleeds for everyone. And, you thank the universe that it is not your children, your wife, or yourself in that car crash, or in that hospital bed dying of cancer.

Sometimes life isn't fair. I wish I could've been able to say "hello" and "goodbye" to my friend. This is what I write back to his wife, and I send my deepest sympathy.

I step out of the café, into the sunlight. As I walk toward my cottage, I begin to absorb all that life is offering me. I notice that I'm surrounded by lush growth and vivid colors. I am overwhelmed by how exquisite each visual of the day has become. Each leaf, tree, cloud is mesmerizing. I am flush with wonderment.

I realize that even the dirt I'm walking on is beautiful. I never thought of this road way before, but the rich dirt I am walking on is beautiful! I'm so glad to share this space with the world. I'm happy to be healthy, to be hungry, to write poems, to desire a woman and to ache for her love. I am happy to surf, to walk the beaches, to share my thoughts and words with others, to be alive, to laugh, and to cry.

And I am crying! I realize huge tears are racing down my cheeks. Oh, I am sobbing from somewhere deep in my heart! Geez, I haven't sobbed with such intensity in years. I can't control the tears!

After a few moments, compose myself, and cry out again. I can't remember crying so hard. What a release! I feel so bad, that this feels good! I am crying for my friend, and I am crying for all my friends and family, those who mean so much to me. The tears are flowing to calm my ache for all I deeply love in my life. Wow, time to let my emotions go! I am letting the tears flow so my insides can call out to the heavens. Scream out to the heavens! I must have been holding a lot of ache inside myself for long time. I must be flushing out all the emotions that I have kept in check for too long! I am crying because it feels so damn good to cry!

It takes me all afternoon to get back to the cottage. It's good to be here. I've become familiar with this space and it feels comfortable to be home. After such a day of emotion, I feel at peace. In fact, I feel amazing, and full of energy! My friend's death has been a rebirth for me. I'm so thankful for all that I have, and all that the world presents to me! I'm enormously grateful to be alive.

I eat dinner like I haven't eaten for days. All sorts of inspirational ideas and aspirations are in my grasp. I sit down at the computer and start writing.

ITALY

The sun is setting, and only nature's brush could paint a sky with such a magnificent array of reds, blues and purples. It is easy to smile in such a lavish atmosphere.

This evening, I notice that I'm not alone. I realize that from the other side of the restaurant, you are also watching the sun drop off the end of the earth into evening bliss. And, you are strikingly beautiful! For the last month, I've been writing quite a lot of verse about women, but there hasn't been much of the feminine gender strolling around...but this evening, a mystery woman arrives on this lost coast.

I approach you and introduce myself.. Your polite "good evening" has an elegant Italian accent. Ah…an Italian, and an Italian beauty, I might add! You tell me that some friends have lent you their beach cottage for a week.

One of the most highly energetic and amazing aspects of this world is infatuation, and I can't help myself, I am totally infatuated! As we say goodnight, and as suavely as possible, I manage to arrange a beach walk for us tomorrow morning.

I've been sleeping extremely well as of late, but tonight, I'm having a difficult time finding slumber. Just two hours earlier, and my life was uncomplicated. And then, a simple introduction to an engaging femme, and wham! What a powerful effect women have on me, and of course, on most men!

The following morning I try to put your arrival in perspective. I think, perhaps this new woman will be a friend for a few days and nothing more. My vivid imagination creates scenarios that may work fine in one of my poems, but these scenarios may not necessarily work in real life.

My reasoning quickly floats away when we meet at the beach, and I see you are wearing the latest, and tiniest, Italian bikini this side of the Mediterranean! I almost burst out laughing! Should I ask if you are wearing this swimsuit (or hardly wearing this swimsuit) to drive me wild!!

After showing you some great coves and beaches, I find that besides beauty, you have brains, intellect and humor. It greatly pleases me to be near such a woman.

The nicest part of our morning together is that we become friends. It's refreshing to share with you, and your stories are eloquent and straight from your heart. You speak from the soul, and I am listening! There is no way to get away from your good looks, but the "woman within you" is getting to me just as much as those lips.

You want me to share some of my poetry, so I suggest that I make you dinner at my cottage this evening. Let the night unfold and maybe we will read some poetry.

I love preparing dinner for a woman! I enjoy the intimacy of creating a warm romantic atmosphere, serving fine wine, and feasting on well prepared, healthy food. I feel comfortable in my surroundings, so hopefully the lady will feel at home in this setting. Women need to be wined and dined, and they need to be nurtured, so wine them, and dine them, and nurture them!

We drink, eat and laugh for a couple of enchanting hours. Daylight has diminished and candlelight puts a soft glow over your skin. We are holding hands when you ask about my writing. I open a journal of unfinished work and you silently read two of my poems, one about spirit, and the other about surfing. You smile as you start to recite the third poem; an adventurous, sensual piece of writing about wild and tender loving. I stop you, take the page from you, and start over. I feel that poetry has to be read and recited with drama and passion.

After I put lots of heart into my presentation, you respond with letting some breath escape from your mouth, and whisper a soft and sensual "oo."

This is all we need to fall into each other's arms. In the candlelight, my hands rest on the warmth of your lower back, your lips are wild with savage hunger, and our kisses are full of tender glory. This is all pure poetry….

Life on this coast just changed from lone walks on the beach, to sharing spectacular hours with a dazzling woman. A new adventure has opened its petals!

BEAUTY

a straw-hat breeze pushed you into my arms
the siren's trance of a healing woman
thank you sweetheart
you swept away all memories of betrayal and loneliness
drama and damage perished forever
I wandered for eternities in search of a stirring femme
we found each other with a simple glance
together, all the alluring senses have come alive
we travel on an ignited avenue of craving
ravishing each other with steamy kisses
seizing one another's body like there is no tomorrow!

ah, tonight's rising moon fascination
creative moonlight
mischievous midnight
delightful, delicious, hypnotic kisses
souls together snuggle and spoon
such a persuading caress
silky sacrifice of clothing
skin to skin
my wild jewel
roll your love over on top of me!

I welcome this sexy dream
splash your wicked sins on me
addictive, pleading scent of desire
magically, you sigh, smile and sway
dance your taboo over my life
your samba has me ablaze!

my lover, what an atmosphere you create!
what talent you possess!
you are so convincing!

you understand the secret!
do you know how good you look!
what a luxury you are!
you are a gift of flesh and inspiration
an exotic angel that fell from heaven

I am self-indulgent!
I must plunge
   within
the deep richness of this Venus
   within
this abundance of pure, lush beauty!

SADDLE UP!

Yesterday, I kissed you goodbye. You boarded a jet and left for your home back in Europe. We are to meet at a romantic lake in the north of Italy later this spring.

Instead of dinners at my cottage, I find I'm at the restaurant four out of five nights a week. I just haven't been in the mood to cook lately. It is vastly different with you gone. I have to adjust to the quiet again, and life sans 'woman'. No femme scent or scenery. What am I to do?

Although I am not as 'at peace' as I was before the woman's entrance, her exit has me to search my soul for better understanding of love. I know this last week has stimulated my imagination for more verse and stories. Yes, I can vividly see you naked, naughty and very nourishing! Ah, I better not think about it too much!

Maybe I need something to shake up my world? Perhaps I need some new surroundings? Maybe I should take a short trip somewhere for a few days? A vacation? It might be good to get out of town. I need a new perspective, a new place and new people. I will travel light, and restart the spirit, "the engine," or at least get a tune up. I'll bring surfboard, money, pen and pad. This sojourn gives me something to look forward to.

I decide on taking the jungle bus south for forty kilometers to a well-known surf break.

The bus ride is beautiful. I'm the only American on board, so I am a novelty for the people.

After my arrival, I book a room at a beach-side lodge, and head to the beach. I paddle out into the waves.

There aren't too many surfers in the water so I enjoy medium size surf all afternoon. A few overhead sets do come through, so I'm energized after the surf session.

While out surfing, I say "hello" to a couple of surfers that I had surfed with a decade earlier. Years ago, we shared some excellent surf on a secret island in the South Pacific. It always amazes me that we surfers can be anywhere in the world, and run into someone we know from surfing. I've been camping on a remote beach in Baja, checking a secluded hideaway in Central America, riding waves on a tiny Caribbean island, or shopping in a farmers market in Biarritz, France, and I will run into someone I know from surfing. The tribe is great!

These old surf acquaintances and I are to meet for dinner later. I am already feeling better about life. Sometimes you just have to saddle up and see what's on the next horizon.

ROCK AND ROLL

Dinner is a lively setting. This is a popular location for those that travel, and lots of folks frequent this coast. Tonight's club scene is fine with me, as I have been spending too much time thinking about my beautiful Italian firend. I need some cheering up and welcome the noisy, and fairly drunk crowd.

I'm not much of a drinker, and never have been. When it comes to alcohol, most people would call me a 'light weight'. Tonight is a small exception, and after a fine dinner of a variety of seafood; we are washing it all down with beer and shots of tequila. The night is starting to get a little wild!

There's one of those old jukeboxes in the corner of the bar that's been blasting out good music all night. We have been feasting on great rock music and classic soul sounds for the last hour. Really a fun time! Another great song begins and many of the café's patrons are singing along to the lyrics. I feel like dancing, so I am up and groovin in between tables. I'm probably dancing like a space cadet, but who cares, because the 'firewater' has taken over, I am fully inebriated!

I'm not alone on the dance floor, and one—no, two women are dancing right along with me. They are smiling and really swinging their hips. I think they look like they could be sisters, or maybe cousins. They are really into some wild dance moves, and accidently, their hips knock over a table's drinks. That sets us off with rounds of laughter.

As the evening unfolds, and somewhere in the mixture of laughter, singing, dancing, the sisters, or cousins, whatever they are, decide to take me home. Which they do! Fantasy fantastic! Wow, what a night! This is the best way to get over any heartache, and I don't think of my Italian girlfriend all night!

Morning brings a violent sun and steamy heat to my dim awareness. I don't know how anyone can make drinking a habit.

I stagger down to the ocean and jump in. Oh, yes, there is hope!

The water cure is my way of reinventing myself. I have used this saltwater medicine at some historic times of my life. I can be drifting in and out of love, or dealing with one of life's tragedies, and the ocean can fix it, or at least, make it better. It's my way to clear my mind and spirit.

I end up staying around the town for a week. Because of the arrival of a new swell and bigger surf, the waves near town do get crowded, so with some new friends that I have made this week, we explore some other breaks. I focus on eating healthy, getting plenty of surf exercise, and writing. It's been a good week, and I feel I'm ready to get back to my cottage, the swaying palms, and front porch for early morning tea.

I hope I will be meeting someone special in Italy in a few months, but this is winter and spring is a long way off.

DANCING HAIKU

ouch!

   oo!

      wow!

my goodness!

   yes!

look at the way you move!

   oh my!

      all women should dance like this!

KISS YOU TATTOO

in this moonlight

the two of you are fascinating

melody of a summer night

wrapped in that warm wind

    princess and princess

    woman caressing woman

smooth grace of desire

stargazing partners of a late night trance

       above the clouds

            shadow wind of the moment

midnight kisses in a tavern of urgency

divine union of honey-scented flesh

your smiles taunt and your eyes tease

      you are offering me all of your sweetness

with such an intriguing invitation, I drift on this ocean of seductive sheets

this is such a tasteful language of loving

    all the gathering of senses and sins

as the candle's dripping dance lights our way,

    we celebrate in the depth of this fertile food

you do this so well!

    thorough

       innovative

         thieves of this dreamy story!

Roy

Many exotic birds nestle in the trees around my little piece of paradise. The toucans have a pleasant sound that fills the day. The macaws don't have a sweet sound. They squawk like there is no tomorrow! Not a pleasant noise, but their colorful feathers are so vibrant and so majestic, I'll put up with their squaking.

My grandfather had the same parrot for forty years. The bird had a greyish black hue; his name was Roy. He wasn't the nicest feathered creature, but he had his days of not biting at you. His being difficult was probably because his was a "life behind bars"! As a child, I didn't realize how important, and how necessary it is for birds and all creatures to have their freedom. Just like humans.

We used to feed Roy sunflower seeds. I actually enjoyed his stature, and the way he looked at me. There was no fucking with Roy! He just did his thing.

At night, they would put a cloth over Roy's cage so he could sleep in darkness.

After my grandfather lost his long battle with cancer and passed away, Roy died the very next day. They told me, it was of a broken heart.

Toast!

The surf dropped dramatically this last week. This drop in *surf action* can throw a lot of surfers into turmoil. I've been there before, but with age, I actually understand and respect the nature of the ocean, and its cycles. So, if the waves are not here, I adjust. They will return, and the habit will be rewarded. I, of course, want to be rewarded all the time! I can be more then ready for the next big swell, I just don't worry about it anymore.

With the surf so flat, I often paddle my surfboard. Paddling is a good means of travel on the ocean; you can float into beaches and coves that are not accessible by foot.

A few years ago, I daydreamed about getting involved in the sport of paddleboarding, and I thought I might enter a race or two. I knew that paddling would just add to my surfing lifestyle, so it was a natural ambition to have more quality time on the ocean. But the reality of competing in a paddleboard race eventually became a humbling experience for me…

…it was a clean flat ocean as all set out from Santa Barbara Harbor one morning for a short, five-mile race. What is five miles when I would soon be competing in, and winning the famous Catalina and Molokai races (each greater than twenty miles)! But, within the first ten minutes of the race, a strong breeze picked up and the ocean turned bumpy. I suddenly felt 'seasick'. My thoughts of grandeur soon gave way to realization of not being in shape. Plus, there's some amazing watermen and women out there in the ocean that could easily kick my butt anytime, and anywhere. A few miles out, and I was toast…

Today, I am not racing, I'm paddling my surfboard up the coast. I have discovered a nice beach. No one has walked on this remote slice of sand for a very long time. At this moment, this exact second, nothing is out of place! The patterns of sand that the wind and sea have arranged are textured with absolute proficiency. It is so beautiful! Serene and postcard perfect, this would be a great place to bring Miss Italy!

I've been on my own for sometime, and I wouldn't mind having a special lady to be my best friend. Someone to complete the equation of living on earth. I've been quite infatuated with this lady, but we are on different sides of the world, and who knows what will become of our relationship? Opening my heart to her may just scare her off. Or, she may melt with emotion. Next thing I know, she will be introducing me to her parents. What!!

Today, I'll just enjoy the serenity of this beach today, and let the daydreams unfold. I know it would be nice to share this beach with some woman, if not my Italian friend, maybe another beauty? I'm a man that simply loves women and all the scents and tastes that go along with their femininity. My lady friend is thousands of miles away, and over the years I have become a little pessimistic about the reality of love and relationships. I've had my share of heartache. I have felt the impact of a broken heart. Perhaps scarred from a couple of romances, I've tried not to let some parts of my heart open fully when in a new relationship. Though, my attempt of staying aloof usually doesn't work exceptionally well, I can fall hard like anyone. Maybe deep inside me there is some optimism, and I'd like to be 'in love' with one soulful woman. I know this would be a huge gift from the universe. Maybe she is in Italy or America, or wherever...but because of lost love, I feel it's better to be open for new romance. The 'adventure' makes me feel alive!

You've just read Zo's bar-stool philosophy of understanding women. Go figure.

This beach…

I have been a little lazy lately. The last few nights, I've been driven to keep composing verse. Sometimes, the writing goes on all night. If not written down on paper, my stanzas and stories will be forgotten when I wake the following morning.

This desire to 'create' is the same for any artist that is passionate about their art form. Paint, clay, marble, dance, words; if you feel it, you have to live it. 'Driven' is a good way to say it. There are days that I can't write a clever thing! I'm just a complete blank. I have no real desire to sit down and try to think up anything that stirs the soul. But lately, I can't stop writing.

So here I am, getting comfortable on the sand. There's a satisfying feeling of serenity when one is just about to fall asleep. Nothing seems important; everything is right where it is supposed to be in life. At this moment in time, I have no desire for anything except what is coming next...and with relaxed and easy breath, I fade fast.

LIGHTNING BUGS

At night, when I walk up the path to my cottage, I see the on-and-off twinkle of lightning bugs. These fireflies appear in the rainy season. There's a certain poetry to their flashing. And the Iguanas sure love eating the bugs. These lizards are a wonderful addition to the jungle lifestyle!

The firefliy twinkling reminds me of my early childhood on the east coast of America. I can still see my siblings on a summer's night, collecting the lighted insects in glass jars. Fun evenings! So these bugs are reminiscent of my summers (only a few) back on Long Island, New York.

My grandparents came from Europe at the turn of the century. All, through Ellis Island to settle in New York. I've got my roots, and I am honored to have the blood of the Italian, Russian and Hungarian cultures running through my veins.

My parents moved from Brooklyn, New York to Balldwin (a small beach town on Long Island) before I was born. My father still took the train into the city to work every day, but folks didn't want to raise their family in the city. They thought it vest to have their children to be raised in the 'mellow' of the *Suburbs*.

I really enjoyed my summers on the East Coast, but my winters weren't as pleasant. I can recall a winter's walk home from a neighbor's house, and I was so cold, just absolutely freezing. I was in tears by the time I walked in the door of my home. Of course, my mom (like so many moms) knew how to take care of me. Thanks Mom! My mom was the best!

Summer, on the other hand, was warm and fun. Our days were full of swimming in the Atlantic, ice-cold popsicles, back porch cookouts, adventures off with my brother, and lots of laughter.

When I was eight years old, our family moved to Southern California. My parents were trying to make a better life for the family, and apparently there were many business opportunities available in California. So, with the warm weather beckoning, we packed it up and moved to the golden state. We were told that the streets were lined with gold! I'm not sure about the gold, but after a short adjustment, my entire youth was spent being nurtured in Southern California.

I adjusted quite well out West, and when I was eleven years old I discovered the sport and lifestyle of surfing. Surfing had just made its splash in California, and I was soon part of the youth movement that was taking on this new craze with open arms. It was a cultural revolution.

I spent every possible minute surfing, and the rest of my time spent thinking about surfing! The sport shaped my life. I was hooked, and I have never gotten over the fascination of riding upon a iiquid canvas of nature. Surfing is one of the healthiest things anyone can do! The waves are filled with high energy and incredible spirit, and to *walk on water,* well, it's the greatest!

Surfing was the backbone of my youth. It enhanced my strong communion with nature. I am honored to be able to still share waves with friends and family today.

The lightning bugs from my past seem to still light my life today. I live in the present, and always look forward to the future, but the past certainly shapes my life.

Tonight, I'll leave the lightning bugs for the Iguanas to eat, write a few paragraphs about growing up, and then, prepare a dinner of onions, peppers and herbs sautéed in butter, and mixed with some well-beaten scrambled eggs. Wow, those sautéed onions sure smell good!

RAINBIRD

With the dry season in full swing here, it's getting extremely hot! The lawn that surrounds my cottage had a lush, vibrant, green glow to it for months. has now dried out and turned brown. Although the peninsula gets a hundred inches of moisture in the rainy season, the grass still needs watering this time of year. So because of this necessity, I've been watering the lawn and shrubs by the cottage.

Although I use the hose to get to certain parts of the lawn, I find a sprinkler is the best way to saturate the grass. I just turn a knob, and away it goes. The watering device that I am utilizing is like the sprinklers that were around when I was a youngster. The one I am usind is the type that the *Rainbird Sprinkler Company* of Southern California, made popular in the 60s.

Oranges…

The orange industry was an integral part of California history in the mid 20th century. But, the orange industry finally succumbed to the era of housing development. Homebuilders started imprinting Southern California with housing tracks, and populating the coast and valleys with multitudes of folks. The buyers of these homes came from everywhere, all to the 'land of plenty.'

I can understand why a family that had put years of hard work into the orange crop, figured that they could make much more money by just selling their land to the developers.

The acres and acres of orange orchards became a gold mine for both, the farmers and for the land developers! Many people suddenly had an opportunity to make large sums of money by forgetting about agriculture, and began to grow houses. The building contractors, carpenters, plumbers, etc., all the people, involved were busy making money.

The charisma of those orange orchards quickly disappeared. Orange trees were being cut down and replaced with housing tracks. It sucked! Within a few short years, all the orchids that we played in were all gone. The land subdivided, and new homes were what filled the horizon for miles and miles. Such is the way of the world. The almighty dollar speaks volumes!

Sprinklers...

I'm not sure if other parts of the country had these *Rainbird* sprinklers, but they were very popular in Southern California. The devises were engineered well. They also had a very unique sound when in use. "Ch, ch, ch, ch, ch, ch, ch"...all the way around in one direction, and then a mechanism would change the gear, and send the water back in the direction it came. And, with a "ta, ta, ta, ta, ta" sound. So beside the sprinklers doing an excellent job nourishing the lawns, they also had this unique sound that is forever embedded in my memory.

In the burning warmth of a Southern California summer, lawns were often saturated in the evening. In this way, the daytime heat wouldn't make the water evaporate too fast. Neighbors would turn on their sprinkler systems in the evening, right around bedtime, the kid's bedtime. So, I'd lie there in the dark, and within the evening stillness, I'd hear the ch, ch, ch, ch...and then, the ta, ta, ta, would soon follow.

It seemed like all was right with the world when the sandman was dusting my eyes. The sound of the sprinklers became a poetic and soothing time of my youth.I would drift off into *la-la land* being nurtured by the rhythm of ch, ch, ch, ch...ta, ta, ta, ta....

LOVERS FLY

Macaws fly in pairs. The brilliant colors of their feathers are of startling red, lavish yellow, and a lustrous blue. And, these colors blended well together in such striking fashion! These birds gently restin the branches of the balsa tree next to my cottage. The chatter they raise makes quite a ruckus. Macaw talk is full of emotion and clamor.

I think all this uproarious communication is part of their love dance. They grab at blossoms and bugs, and pass them back and forth to each other, beak to beak, and loudly squabbling the whole time.

A neighbor told me macaws mate for life. They keep the same partner their entire lives! Wow, how romantic! Isn't it wonderful?

So perhaps these macaws are total "love birds," soaring through the sky as spirit friends, and as lovers, representing all that is sacred in life.

Or just maybe…

As these birds are beak to beak, they are just complaining to each other. I mean after so many years of living together, maybe they are just tired of the constant companionship.

I can hear it now, "Here, you so and so, eat it already. What did you say, jeez, always nagging me, what, we never have fun anymore, and what, I'm a lousy provider. Well you never clean up the nest anymore, and the same old scent everyday. When's the last time you got frisky with me?

Hopefully, after a while, these macaws begin to snuggle. They apologize to each, and whisper, "Dear, you mean everything to me, I love you so much."

The grace of love between true soul mates always rings true.

Midnight Comrades

The main focus in my life is to surf, and to enjoy the adventures that accompany wave-riding sojourns. To keep the surf adventures unfolding, I am always open to any grand business idea that might net me some coin and help pay for all the fun. So any enthusiastic entrepreneurial endeavor offered to me is always looked at carefully and as wisely as possible. I'd weigh the investment of time and money, the possible profit, and of course, the risk. This effort was how one might be able to pay rent, and still be able to travel to an exotic desination occationally.

I have a friend that travels throughout Mexico. Whenever he is back in America, he and I always make a point of getting together and saying hello. Back in the States, one evening, he tells me he has some property on this lost coast, on the edge of a wild tropical jungle. He has been working on the piece of land and has plans to construct a dwelling. Besides developing the project, my friend spends as much time possible surfing right in front of his property. *This is a vast stretch of coastline, and the surf is void of any other surfers. I note that Mexico is a gold mine of good waves.* My friend goes on to tell me he needs someone else to surf with and invites me along for an adventure. So without much hesitation, and with very little planning (or money); I find myself in an old Chevy truck heading down mainland Mexico in pursuit of a deserted beach with a good wave, and a whole lot of adventure.

The truck is loaded with our surfboards, food, appliances and televisions. The reason for the kitchen devices is not to mix ingredients for a chocolate cake. And the televisions aren't because of missing a Sunday football game. These products are for trading with pot farmers up in the mountains. You see, my friend and I also plan on scoring some pot and smuggling it back into the States. *Although surfing is the main source of encouragement here, we are living a lifestyle of an era that appeared many decades ago....*

The journey throughout Mexico is always a large undertaking, and one that is saturated with enough stories to fill a few books. Anybody that has made this passage into the "unknown," and even the "known" of Mexico understands the journey can become a pilgrimage—and sometimes even a quest, a mission for warm water, gutsy surf, self-realization, and maybe, sanity. Yes, this can be a hair-raising, desperate undertaking! It's like a marathoner finishing their last five miles of a race. Arriving at your destination is more than satisfying, it can be a God-send.

A couple of thousand miles later, we arrive at our destination. We've rented a small cabin for a few days from an old acquaintance. He tells us the waves at the 'Point' have been head-high, and we should get consistent surf as the swell is building for the next couple of days. This fits into our plans quite well, as it will take a few days to sort out the business end of our sojourn. Our plan: 1) score a large amount of hemp from the farmers that grow herb in the highlands, 2) make a long journey south to my comrade's property, 3) make the stash presentable, 4) transport our package to America.

The surf at the 'Point' is going off, and after the long drive to get here, I am enjoying this quality wave to the max! My friend mentions, that this same swell that we are surfing here should make for some good waves at the river mouth in front of his property.

By the end of the third day, we are told that everything is in place for our score of marijuana. By tomorrow night, we should be eighty kilos of quality hemp richer, or about 175 lbs. in standard measurement.

I should mention, the friend I'm traveling with, tells a good story. His tales are usually a wonderful expressive time at any gathering. He's got the "gift of gab," and that's why I like going on sojourns with him. So rolling into one of his narratives, he mentions that one time, on the back of a mule, when he was traveling into the highlands with his pot connections to make a big score...

So, he's on his way to visit the hemp farmers that he's done business with for the last year. The trail up the mountain is famous for banditos holding-people-up for everything they owned. So his group of local middle-men that he's hired on this wild ride, are armed with guns and rifles. And, they've given him a shotgun to carry. Now if you know my friend, you'd know that he is the last person in the world that knows guns, and shouldn't be holding one. But, aware of the understandable danger, he snuggles his weapon like a veteran.

Luckily, no banditos rob them for the cash. No blasting gunfight arises from the journey. But, somewhere around a hairpin corner on the mountain trail, the mule he sits upon, loses its balance and slips a few feet down an embankment. In the ruckus, the shotgun he's holding on to goes off with the sound of a cannon, and a blast of buckshot just misses a couple of men by inches!

The sound of the blast scares the shit out of himself, the mules, and everybody else. All this commotion is enough to make sure any bandito within five miles knows exactly where the caravan is traveling. With the animal eventually back on the mountain trail, the group continues on its journey up the mountain. My friend can see the other companions just shaking their heads. He can't quite make out what they are saying, he can only imagine! He feels like the total novice, but what did they expect from someone that dropped out of Cub Scouts?

The night of the "score" unfolds…

Our "business" meeting is around midnight. Three men show up, and two of them do the hauling of the pot into the *casita* we are staying. The other fellow is our connection. He is dressed much nicer than the other two, who are in worn out shirts, jeans and old tethered sandals. Our "connection" is wearing a clean, white western shirt, dark polyester pants and cowboy boots. My friend has done business with the well-dressed man a couple times prior to this evening.

Our money is ready to be presented and counted. The televisions and small kitchen appliances are all in sight. All three men look very pleased with the extras we brought to trade. (*These were the days when many remote areas of Mexico didn't have access to the modern conveniences that are so readily available today*). The hemp is looked at carefully, the money is counted and the deal is done. We don't smoke the pot with these people, as this isn't a social gathering, this is business. These people expect that we do have knowledge of the product without smoking it. We do have this knowledge, and we do understand the nature of this business. There is plenty of time to get high. We shake hands with the one "main" fellow, and say goodbye. One of the big televisions is a source of conversation during the transaction. I think all three men want it.

We watch the headlights of their truck disappear into the blackest of evenings. Around here there are no streetlights that brighten the nighttime sky. There are no cities or highways close by, just darkness and thick jungle to accompany my story.

After a few moments, my friend picks up two of the bags and tells me to accompany him with the other couple of bags of weed. We head off into the jungle, quite a distance from our place, and hide the stash in a safe spot that we had located a day earlier. We then make our way back to the *casita*, blow out the candles, and wait. The reason for this precaution is that one never knows if the *Federales* (the cops) have been tipped off about our business endeavor. Many a deal can go awry here, and all over the planet, because someone wasn't on the 'up-and-up.'

This is probably the most stressful time of my trip so far. I hate the idea of a local police knocking at our door and giving us the third degree. Luckily, the night is empty of any surprises, and we get some sleep.

We are up early, and we load the large bags of hemp on a local kid's eighteen-foot canoe. This young surfer is a good friend of ours. He told his father (it's his dad's canoe) that he is going fishing. We're glad he's assisting with hauling our stash down the coast, some eight kilometers away. He knows we will reward him generously for his part in the transport.

This journey would take hours by car or bus, but traveling *incognito* in this boat with a 25 horsepower engine, we should complete this trip within an hour. The alternative to a boat would be using the jungle bus that takes locals along the coast from one town to another. This would be an exhausting experience. I've been on the bus a few times and it's a whole adventure onto itself.

After getting through the shore's wave, the boat ride down the coast is beautiful. We motor in deep water, some four hundred meters off the coastline, so we aren't worried about any ocean swells making for a rough ride. Looking at land from a boat is always a fascinating experience. It is easy for one to feel removed from all that is on land…one just floats along in life. And the jungle is quite stunning from this distance. There is so much of it!

After a pleasant hour's ride, we round the corner of a bay and are nearing our final destination. Our plan is to aim for a safe beach where we are to unload everything. We tell the young man steering the boat to go straight toward the beach. Now, he's aware of how to bring a vessel onto the sand, but with us wanting to be careful with our merchandise, we tell him anyway. We don't want the boat turning perpendicular to the waves near the shore. Straight in, and resting on the sand is the only way to navigate this, as turning sideways to the oncoming waves could prove hazardous!

Our next few minutes are filled with urgency and chaos as the motor starts *puttering*. The darn thing has been going strong the entire voyage down here, and all of a sudden it is in trouble…and so are we, because in the next couple of seconds, the engine quits completely, and the canoe starts drifting off course! Sure enough, we turn sideways to the shore and a threatening wave that has a big enough of a surge to take us right over on our side and upside down, does! We tumble over, and all aboard, plus the cargo, are in the *drink*. Talk about a comedy of errors!

We do our best to grab the bags of pot from getting soaked with salt water. Luckily, we did take the time to take the stash out of the large canvas bags they came in. We wrapped them in a couple of layers of plastic garbage bags, anticipating just some type of mishap as has just occurred. What a good way to ruin a promising business venture!

We all end up soaked, but our 175 pounds of pot is intact and not damaged. I don't care if our clothing and food supply may be somewhat ruined, but our business investment is important. Actually the food is important, and we salvage what we can.

We are safe because the rice was kept in air-tight plastic containers for protection from any bugs that love getting into such things in tropical climates. No salt water got in the containers. We weren't carrying much in the way of supplies because we knew we'd be eating local fruit and a good amount of fresh fish.

After regrouping on the sand, we wave to our departing friend. I hope the outboard motor doesn't give him any more trouble on his return voyage.

Now we make haste, and take everything off the beach, through the jungle and onto the shore of a river. With the aid of a canoe we will cross the river and set up a make-shift *palapa* (dwelling) on a beach. Here we will get the pot in *sellable* shape. We will have to manicure the cuttings, and make sure the buds are ready for buyers. There's also the question of getting all this hemp back across the border to America.

Our idea is to hire a pilot we know, and have him fly down, grab our stash and deliver it to California. We are to meet our pilot and plane at a secluded jungle landing strip. The whole affair of the plane landing and taking off should only take twenty minutes. Our pilot does this type of smuggling often, and he knows where to stop for fuel without having to answer many questions from the local officials. Some of these officials may need to be persuaded with some money, but that is the way of this land and its officials. Because of the risk, the pilot will do very well financially. He will get paid after our product is sold back in the U.S. His mission is to fly very low toward California, and to eventually arrive at an airstrip in a remote section of California desert. As I mentioned he's a seasoned pilot and scammer, so he is into the profit, and the heightened adrenaline of the risk. He does this transporting of pot a few times a month with his many connections in the business. But our plan with the pilot, plane and desert are a week or two away, so now, is the time to start constructing our place to sleep and work here on this beach.

During our first day's tasks, we will look toward the waves ever so often and think about going surfing. It's understood, that we'll have plenty of time for surfing after we get settled into a daily routine. Remember, work and play is what this trip is all about!

By day two, we settle into a life of riding surf, and of spending hours *cleaning* our product. The temperature is so damn warm here that we surf for a few hours first thing in the morning. It's usually at daybreak, because as the day goes on, the sun's intensity can be too heavy, almost unbearable! We spend the rest of our day going through the weed making it ready for transport.

We take our time with preparing the dinner meal of rice and whatever fish we catch each day. One of us will take to fishing in the afternoon. We have gone a day without catching anything, and then it's rice, and that is usually coconut rice. We augment our meals with fresh fruit that we pick in the nearby jungle. We sometimes work on cleaning the pot at night, but working in the daylight gives us a much better perspective on the product than at night by candlelight.

One week on the beach, and into our adventure, and we are ready to get the plane down here for exporting. We are also ready to get off this beach and rid ourselves of the uncomfortable feeling of being sandy all the time! Both, my buddy and myself enjoy *roughing* it, but this is certainly extreme! What I am saying is that the novelty of the beach life is wearing thin. We've been somewhat uncomfortable because of the lack of fresh water to wash the constant feeling of being "sandy" off of our skin. Give me a clean bed and a hot shower any day! We are also ready for a different variety of food. We do get our share of fun surf the entire week. It is great to be in surf shape and tan. I feel sharing good waves with a friend is a kinship of spirit. Just hooting and hollering at each other's rides will create some lasting memories, and some good surf stories!

After all our work is complete, my friend makes the bus ride back to a nearby town. There, he will phone our pilot and set everything in motion. I didn't volunteer to make the bus ride. Waiting alongside a jungle path in the middle of nowhere, and for hours, isn't the fun! The long wait is because one is never quite sure of the bus schedule, its mechanical reliability, or of jungle's road conditions. While my friend takes on this chore, my job is to make sure all's secure around our campsite.

After the constant companionship for a couple of weeks, this being by myself is nice. Without the company of someone else here, I have no one to communicate with except the birds and creatures of the jungle. So, obviously, not much conversation is going on. I keep myself busy by writing in my journal. I have always been a writer, and I find the sharing of truth and fiction has an appealing aspect of using my time wisely. Some people read, some paint, some cook, some sit in front of a TV…I write.

After my friend's return to the "business and cultural" center we built here at the beach, we share a few laughs around the campfire. The following morning we surf our last waves together here at our little surf mecca. We then tear down the camping area, clean, and pack what is necessary. We load our large bags of cleaned and ready-to-market pot on some mules that we have rented from a local rancher. We've made arrangements to leave his animals at his relative's ranch after our need for their use is over. The ranch is not far from the hidden landing strip we will be using.

All this cloak and dagger stuff is stimulating for our imaginations. Our burst of inspiration may also be from getting off the beach and onto our next step in our scheme to become rich. We also stash our surfboards in the sand, hoping to retrieve them on a future surf safari. They are not part of our exit plan as we are traveling as light as possible.

Our trip through the jungle is not an easy one. I'm glad the animals are carrying the burden of all the weight. We become exhausted because the journey is rough, dirty, and bug filled. We also feel drained because the jungle is so thick and dense with foliage that we have been constantly swinging our machetes to stay on the path. We had anticipated more time was going to be needed for this part of the excursion, and told the pilot to give us more time till we arrive at the airstrip. The trip ends up taking us an extra day of travel time to get to our rendezvous spot.

In the vicinity of the airstrip, we hide the load of weed, and return the animals to the ranch to which we agreed. We then return to the airstrip and get everything ready for transport. We wait in a fairly removed section of the runway, so as not to be seen or heard. Funny, did I write, "fairly removed"? Jeez, this whole fucking jungle is "removed" from everything! This is such an intense environment that I find myself daydreaming about my small, clean and comfortable home back in California. There's nothing like a hot bath, soft towel, a full refrigerator, and a comfortable bed to put a smile on my face. All of us are into our own comfort zone, and right now I am thinking about that 'zone"'in California! I'll be living that daydream soon enough, so I better stay focused.. Although, there is nothing wrong with letting the mind wander a little, especially here in the middle of nowhere.

I can't believe how everything in our adventure is working out so smoothly, because after two hours of waiting by the runway, we hear our friend's plane through the silence of the heat. It is amazing that with so much happening in the last couple of weeks, our schedule has been working so efficiently.

We move onto the runway and signal him with a wave as he passes over. Within minutes, he has landed his plane. I am again amazed, because these *bush pilots* can land a plane in the craziest places. This is a very short runway!

The pilot climbs out of his plane, and acts like it's just another day of finding a parking place at the neighborhood grocery store. We greet him with a handshake and some praise for his taking care of his end of our endeavor with such efficiency. He's friendly, and also professional about our next part of the transport. He asks about the poundage he is carrying back, and he then repeats the next few steps of our plans that he's agreed to. We carefully load the pot aboard, and then all three of us climb into the plane and fasten our seatbelts, and we are off! I look out the window of the small plane. Wow, the jungle looked grand from a boat, but it is even more beautiful and exotic from the air!

The plan is for my comrade-in-arms and myself to be dropped off at another airstrip that is fairly close by. From that location, and a two-hour bus ride later, we will be at an international airport. We will then get on a commercial flight bound for California. All our travel time is to coincide with our pilot's arrival time at an airstrip out in the California desert. This timing should prove to be the tricky part of our plan, but hopefully tomorrow night, after our return flight home and our renting a car, we will be loading the pot into the trunk of that car.

The flight back to America is wonderful! This sure beats my last couple of weeks of discomfort by a mile. And the tequila I am sipping, has put a soft glow on everything. I slip into slumber and the next thing I hear, is that we are descending toward our arrival city in California.

We land, deplane, go through U.S. Customs, and grab our rental car. It will be somewhat of a long drive toward the desert, but we are on a mission. So without much conversation, we drive.

As we continue our journey into the sandy backdrop of the desert landscape. I think to myself, that there's just as much desert as there was jungle. Hopefully, all will continue as well with since our venture started. All good adventures need a good ending!

We eventually get to our desert airstrip, and the general spot where we are to meet the plane. This is certainly no-man's-land! I mean there isn't anything here. We are in the middle of nowhere! Not a tree in sight, just sand and cactus. I thought the jungle was an endless sea of green, this desert has the same feeling, but tan and dry.

And it's quiet, really quiet! It almost feels strange to disturb the quiet with one's own voice. Very different than the jungle where you hear toucans, parrots, monkeys, and some strange sounds that you can't quite put to any specific creature. The desert is void of these sounds—it is only stillness. And the air is very dry! I focus on how dry it is, and I realize that my sinuses are perfectly clear. The tropical moisture that I was accustomed to for the last few weeks is not present. This breathing in of the dry desert air feels good.

Now we wait. And we wait. And we wait! In fact, we eventually start getting nervous when four hours pass with no sign of the pilot, plane, or the cargo! We make a few comments wondering on why he isn't here yet. We try to stay positive and not throw any negative thoughts into the equation. Hopefully, there is just some minor delay in the final hours of his flight.

I think to myself about an account of a similar situation someone told me of some years earlier...

This fellow was waiting for his pilot, plane and load of pot to arrive just as we are waiting in tonight's shadows for our shipment. But the plane's arrival and the scenerio didn't turn out well! The entire affair turned ugly! After the plane landed and the engine was turned off, the Mexican police drove out of the bushes and onto the runway...guns-a-blazing! The pilot was killed and the pot was confiscated. My acquaintance watched the whole affair from a mile away through binoculars. He escaped without getting pinched by the cops, but he lost quite a lot of money. Plus the reality of the gunfire and the death of the pilot rattled him to the core. This nightmare all happened across the border, back in Mexico, where those situations can arise.

This is America, and guns may be drawn, but there wouldn't be any gunfire. The real scenario is that the entire fiasco would cost thousands of dollars in legal fees, and months of hassle to be resolved.

I don't even want to go there, and I don't mention the episode to my friend! I go back to thinking about home, a woman in that bathtub, and this hair-brain scheme being over. We just patiently sit and wait another hour…here in the middle of nowhere.

These moments of reflection are good for the soul. It is a nice wake-up call to focus on some other aspect of life that's better then importing pot for consumption. And that is exactly why people are in this pot business…it is for other people's consumption. It's grown, sold, and smoked. A plant that people want, will pay money for, and some people will even risk their freedom to be involved with it as a business. And that's why I'm in a car in the middle of a desert right now!

I'm getting way too serious. I probably need to smoke a bit of bud! I decide a joke would be appropriate. A couple of jokes later, and some shared laughter, my buddy and I are feeling better about everything. We both comment that this has been quite an adventure so far! We extend our hands and share a strong handshake. We've shared in this sojourn as comrades…midnight comrades!

Another hour, and as the sun slowly begins to rise, we hear the faint sound of what could be an airplane. Somewhere, off in the distance, we see a plane on the horizon? Maybe? Yes? Fantastic, it is a plane, and it's fast approaching! And it is our plane! Happy day!

A few minutes later, the airplane descends, and touches down on the runway. The only sound is that of the plane's engine, it pleasingly purrs through the desert silence….

ABANDONED HOUSE

I wandered upon the beach for an hour this morning. I drifted in and out of the shallow water. Eventually, I came upon an abandoned dwelling up off the sand, about fifty meters into the jungle. It was a bamboo structure with a palm-thatched roof. It had a haunting appeal.

I could see the cottage looked like it hadn't been occupied for some time. Probably years earlier, an adventurous couple looked out from the structure,, and toward the ocean, and figured that they were living in paradise.

Today, this cottage looks like it'd have a sign on the door that reads, "No one home, this dream is over." The bamboo home had no friendly faces looking out, toward the sea. Maybe, it's the jungle that got to the inhabitants. Just, too intense. This house will probably be part of the jungle flora soon enough. The *jungle* has its way.

This uninhabited structure triggers a memory of my strolling down a street that I'm familiar with back in California…

While walking, I notice a store with a sign in the window that reads, "Out of Business." The store's doors just didn't open that day.

To me, this sight has sadness attached to it. The business endeavor was probably a huge part of somebody's life at one time. The store, was once, a wonderful dream. A good investment. The enterprise was going strong with sales one spring and bubbling with customers, and then, as the months passed, it lost its glamour with the public. With funds dwindling, the owners realize they can't afford to keep the shop going. A great business one year, and then the next year, not so strong, and it's gone.

I think of all those dreams of having a thriving enterprise go belly-up. All the optimism, shattered. There's always a good month of sales and more hope…only to have the next month's reality of too many bills, and not enough money to pay them, come thundering back. Consequently, the doors are locked, the bright lights are turned off, and the space is empty.

The pleasant ending to this story, is that after being vacant for sometime, the store's space is suddenly a beehive of activity with new owners, and a new dream. As I walk by, I can see carpenters are now working in a space that appeared so empty. And toward the back of the store, an architect is looking over drawings while a young couple are pointing here and there, enthusiastically explaining their concepts to the architect. These new business owners are full of optimism and zeal! A new dream is unfolding! Another *new beginning* is becoming a reality.

This gives me hope. I understand that there are beginnings, and there are endings, and those endings can be a terrible time in one's life, but there's reason to believe in a happy ending. Everyone has visions of a bright future.

Today, here on the beach, I feel this abandoned bamboo house has seen better days. I think it'd be better to just let the jungle have it back.

And maybe, one day, some folks will buy the property, build a home and hang a sign on the door that reads, " Welcome Friends."

Salt Water Skin

The waves have been running strong and fierce these last couple of weeks. This is the season when the stronger swells begin, so the larger surf has created a new excitement in the air.

After months of small surf, the larger waves are welcome. Some people only surf for the *big wave rush*. I've never considered myself a big wave enthusiast. I just want to draw lines on a clean canvas of water. Just have fun! There is nothing I have to prove to myself in riding intense, triple-overhead, giant surf. Surfing a well-shaped wave that grinds along a headland (an ocean point) is all I need to satisfy my surf obsession. This takes care of my surf addiction just fine. Though, I agree; riding a big wave can be very exciting! It's quite a rush!

I ride a point wave that is within walking distance of my cottage. I simply paddle around a small, rocky peninsula to the *take-off* spot. I usually surf for hours, and then take a break on the beach. I recharge with food and water, and then get back out in the waves. This surf spot is not a secret, but most traveling surfers hit a few of the better-known surf breaks that are further down the coast. Luckily, the location where I surf is not the main break in town, so it never has too many surfers in the lineup. I don't like crowded surf at all! A crowd can change the vibe in the water. It doesn't have to be this way, but crowds do breed a survival attitude.

I enjoy sharing waves with only a couple of surfers. And, I like applauding others that are getting good waves. So a feeling of camaraderie is usually enhanced with only a few surfers in the water. I also enjoy surfing with women.

Women just add to the grandness. There are some men that don't like sharing the surf with women. These surfers also tend to complain about standup surfers, boogie borders, knee boarders and bodysurfers. They also have a negative comment if they think your board is too long or too short! I have no time for these people. What foolishness! I can't imagine someone complaining about sharing waves with women? My outlook is women and surfing are the two ways to enter through the pearly gates, and into heaven!

Besides using my surfboard for my go-outs, bodysurfing has been included in my daily ocean fun. In this warm water it's easy to spend hours in the water, And, with the aid of swim fins it's easier to catch waves when bodysurfing.

Before most of us ever tried board surfing, we bodysurfed the waves. And today, using your body has become a vision of grace and style. The whole concept of being in the curl without any type of board to *plane* on is spiritually and physically enhancing. I have also found that thirty minutes of bodysurfing feels like I have been swimming two miles! Actually ,sprinting two miles. So the workout, the finesse, and fun are my reasons of why I enjoy the sport. Bodysurfing is a beautiful art form, and it means more quality time splashing around in the ocean!

On the beach, it feels 'native' to let the salt water dry on my skin. That salt water feels healthy, and it promotes the lifestyle. I mean, down here, this world is supposed to dry on your skin. You have to let the atmosphere touch you and seep within your soul.

SURF HAIKU

the ride

     the slide

         the glide

     life in liquid

SECRET SPOT

Most every day, two local kids watch as I surf. I wave to them from the water, and they wave back. So, I've adopted Gregory and Thomas as my beach buddies.

If I lose my board in the surf and have to swim for it, they are there as surfboard caddies. Big smiles on their ten-year-old faces as they retrieve my board.

I know they want to try surfing, so two surf addicts are in the making.

Eventually, I do decide to take them under my wing and introduce them to the good life. Each youngster takes a turn with the surfboard. We walk into the ocean as far as we can go without their heads going under the sea's surface. I'll then settle one on top the surfboard, and push the board toward the beach. And as the surfboard gathers momentum, they jump to their feet, and ride toward shore. They're both doing quite well, and having lots of fun.

I've met their parents and the rest of their large families. Good people.

Recently, the boys started bringing their seven-year-old sister, Carlota, to the beach with him. It's understood, the older children take care of younger siblings around here.

We all make sure Carlota is safe and amused on the sand. She wants her turn on the surfboard soon.

+++

Most weekends, the boys and their family go ten kilometers north to their uncle's banana farm. Upon their arrival, they spend a couple of days assisting their extended family work the farm.

The boys tell me I should accompany the family, and surf the waves near the property.

Now these kids don't know a lot about waves and how a set-up might look for good surfing, but they are enthusiastic, so I agree to the escapade. One never knows, maybe there is "the secret surf spot" just ten kilometers away!

There's a road that connects our town to where the banana farm lies. Though, I wouldn't call it an actual road! It's more of a washed-out path through the jungle, and barely wide enough to accommodate the open-air bus. Luckily, the bus is constructed with vacant siding and a canopy roof which assist in circulating the hot, tropic air in this jungle environment.

Slowly, we make are way through the jungle's dense forest. The trip is long and bumpy! It's difficult to believe that the family makes this journey most every weekend!

Ultimately, we reach our destination. My two surf caddies are gong-ho, and my surfboard is the source of necessity for the boys to carry. Consequently, I make sure it's under my arm so not to get damaged.

After a short walk, we come upon a clearing and there, I view the beginning of the banana orchard. Acres and acres of banana plants cultivate the area. I see why this is a family run operation!

Thomas's father and his brother (the boy's uncle) have been working the farm for many years, and they seem to make a good living from their hard work. They are far from rich, but compared to many people in this country, they do well.

Everyone greets me warmly, and we have a bit of food before the family turns to work. I offer my assistance, but I'm their guest and they wouldn't think of having me labor.

They insist that I explore the beach, and Carlota, the perfect seven-year-old hostess, grabs my hand and escorts me toward the beach. A couple of her young cousins accompany us. I am the new kid on the block and they are thrilled to have me here.

We don't walk too far till I hear the sound of the surf. This resonance always makes me feel alive!

Our group then walks through an opening in the jungle, and we view the sea. My jaw drops in amazement as I see a picture-perfect wave zip across the bay! Lines of well-groomed waves rap around a headland, and spin across the point! What a vision!

Carlota and her cousins take to playing in the sand. The children don't understand why I'm so awe-struck, but they know something significant is happening!

I'm smiling as I paddle out. This is a warm tropical sea, and the waves are absolutely dreamy! I'm here by myself, and this feels like Christmas morning!

The waves are consistent and slightly overhead in size. It's a quick take off, and then I'm carving turns along the wave's blue canvas! Each section of the surge is stout and groomed! Some of the curls expand into sweet, tight tubes! I can't believe the luck! What a place!

After a while, I notice Thomas and Gregory are on the beach with the other kids. I knowledge their presence. I look forward to thanking the boys for encouraging me to come along!

All the children eventually head back to the farm. I surf for another solid hour. No other humans in sight. I'm solo, and at a perfect secret surf spot!

Perhaps it's the combination of the physical exercise and the chemical reaction ignites the endorphins, but this type of surf session puts one in a spiritual state of consciousness. Right now, I am flying high!!

It's always wonderful to be upon the ocean, but riding high-quality waves becomes a true cosmic experience! Here I am trying to explain it, and it can't be explained, it has to be lived.

I am wondering if this location has a title. Perhaps it's christened with a saint's surname.

Maybe, I'll name this site, Lorenzo's? Yeah, Point Lorenzo! Though, that doesn't sound appropriate as I'm only a guest here. I don't have the birthright to claim it for my own.

I have a grand proposal. I'll call it "Point Carlota"!

Someday, wave-hungry surfers will make bold safaris to ride Point Carlota! And dozens, upon dozens of embellished narratives will enhance the legendary break!

And in time, someone will buy the location and begin the process of creating a "surf resort". They will construct a hotel, hire the locals to cook and clean, and charge surf-enthusiasts $4,000 a week to ride this surf break.

The guests will be wined and dined, and surfed out! The surf magazine will print exclusive stories and spectacular images that will enhance the legendary break! A larger-than-life fantasy, no one will be able to resist Point Carlota!

Yes, bought, ravished and fucked! I'm glad I got here when I did!!

I make my way off the beach, and back to my hosts and the afternoon's meal preparation. I hope they let me assist with the task.

WAVES OF DREAMS

January clings to the cold
transfer to tranquil warmth

I see a thoughtful moon in a tropic sky
it graces my visit with a celebration of the winter solstice
    another Christmas morning, and the dawning of a new year
waves of dreams have arrived with a new swell

blue
blue ocean
your grasp charms me
your rhythm gathers in my core
   and forever marches upon the shore of my life
you grace my skin
   and you seep within my world
this ocean wisdom
it cleanses and purifies my life
   my focus
it gives me strength and substance

living the dream is where I want to be!

surf is exploding all around me
    howling offshore winds transcend the face of each wave
    I am greeted with grand sets of Pacific surf
    water showers over and upon me
    each stunning blissful second is pure brilliance!

I use deep strokes to paddle into the wave's energy
as the surge picks me up, I stand
   speeding downward
      downward
   off the bottom and to carve a turn
I love this first turn!

shifting momentum has me climbing the face of the wave
I move toward the wave's holy ground, the pocket!
   the tube!
     so profound!
bliss and blessing!

this canvas grows longer and longer
     section after section
big turns
body extending and compressing
  standing tall and proud
gracefully trimming
touching the wave's face
   it's a dance!
weighting and de-weighting
    all in the knees
    all in the body positioning
it's all harmony
I have to sing my own song
   it would be foolish to be anything more than myself

the profound essence of surfing
this ultimate blend of my life gliding on this surface of water
   in this exact moment
     on a stage of surf
       my spirit is set free!

Surprise!

Your visit takes me by surprise. I would never expect to see the woman that I lived with years earlier to show up in such a remote coast.

You tell me that you've been traveling with girlfriends and you were only an hour away, so you left your companions to see me for a day. I think you have something important to say, something to get off your chest, as some parts of our breakup never got resolved. You tell me that's not the reason for this surprise hello. You got over your anger years ago. You just wanted some space from your friends.

For me, it is odd having you here, and it's difficult to think of the past and act like we are comfortable with everything. Our last few months of living together weren't pleasant. I have moved on, but this just doesn't feel right. You sense this and suggest a drink or a joint. You think we need to let our hair down and laugh.

I figure the ocean is a cure-all, and invite you for a swim. As we walk down to the beach, I think to myself that maybe you just came here to have sex. Married or not, you always had a burning desire to make love. You have now been away from your husband for a week, and you are probably just horny.

We always had great sex. We explored each other to the max, and we always fulfilled our desires with great intensity. So, although I am wishing that you were my Italian lady friend, I think your visit will be beneficial for me. Jeez, I have a one-track mind! Maybe we do need a drink or smoke to laugh about the whole thing!

We take a swim and then sit in the shallow water and talk. I see you have grown in your outlook on life. This ocean is very warm, so sitting here is a good way to relax and spend the afternoon.

I bring down some drinks and snacks, and we lay in the water so long that our skin starts to *prune*. Eventually, we have to get out of the sun, so we head back to the cottage.

We shower off in the outside shower, and you keep your swimsuit on throughout the shower, but when we step inside the cottage, you strip to pink nakedness. As you towel yourself dry, you give me that *look*, and ask if I am also going to get naked! With an afternoon of sun, drinks, and a fresh shower, your pinkness looks good enough to devour. I pull off my trunks and take you in my arms. We drift toward the bedroom. We almost don't make the bed because of how carried away we get. This is how our early years of being together were, as we made spectacular love twenty-four-seven!

After being away from you for so many years it is very exciting to be underneath, on top, within, and around every inch of you. You have stayed firm and your sexuality has not diminished at all. You take and give, the way considerate lovers should take and give.

Later, after our indulgence in sharing such lustful lovemaking, we rest in the warmth of the late afternoon void. We are wrapped in each other's arms for a short time, but now the day's heat has pushed us to different ends of the bed. We are both thinking about what just happened.

I tell you it pleases me to have your wetness, and its scent on my skin and lips. And it does! You are silent, but smiling. I wonder why you came all this way to see me.?Maybe I'm correct, and you just needed a shot of sex.

I surprise you and grab a powerful bud of pot and small pipe from the dresser drawer. This sure seems like as good a time as any to get stoned!

We do take a couple of tokes each, and we are soon giggling about nothing in particular. Our stories then become exaggerated and we are now laughing, sometimes almost uncontrollably. I know I am "out there," and you seem the same. We've had a lot of fun this afternoon.

We eventually get *sexy-eyes* for each other and we start making out. I love good kissing; it is such an aphrodisiac for high-gear sex. Another round of fabulous lovemaking, and we are worn out.

Over dinner at the café we discuss our lives after living together. We both have moved on very well. I have'nt brought up your husband, and I don't plan to. If you talk about your marriage, I will listen. Maybe this is a bad time in your relationship and you have parted from each other? Maybe this is a great time of your marriage and you just felt like making love to me? You don't talk about the marriage, so we talk about a few of our old friends.

After dinner and a short session of kissing, we fall asleep. In the morning you quickly pack, and you are all business. That is not a good way to explain your attitude or disposition, but you got what you came for, and a job well done.

We have a sweet embrace, kiss and say goodbye, and you then drive off.

THE SWEET SMILE ON YOUR FACE

my love
there is the sweetest smile on your face
you are so aroused
so alive
embracing your passion
embracing your beauty
I love seeing you this way

there is a wild look in your eyes
an eager savage touch as you lean into a kiss
your desires set free
your lush imagination
tempted
unlocked
untamed

you lavishly take, and give
such delight in your exploration
such strength
such sensuality

dreamy rhythm conquest
surrendering to the woman within
you capture that sweet treasure
your joyous release
such a sacred sacrament of your power
the richness of your soaking celebration
magic in the banquet of your ecstasy

your spirit lifted
you glow in a saga of mysterious raw energy
your true nature set free

I respect how necessary this is for you
I honor this wild gift that you share with me

with that sweet smile on your face
you parade like Eve in the Garden of Eden
and like Adam, I will eat anything you offer

The Heart of a Tortoise

The waves haven't been marching through lately. Though, some teaser sets do march, but even those waves have no punch. No gusto, no get-up-and-go! It's also has been raining non-stop for a few days. Life just gets better when the sun is out, and when the surf is pumping!

Awake and moving about the cottage at sunrise, I decide to walk down to the beach and check the surf. With my surfboard under my arm, I am ready for any type of surf session.

On the beach, I see some suspicious, odd-looking imprints in the sand. These huge tracks have come from the ocean, and are off the beach some yards. The impression in the sand looks like a large truck has driven here, leaving its tire tracks.

These large tracks upon the sand remind me of the same impressions that elephant seals leave on the beaches back in California. It now dawns on me that these tracks on the sand are from a large tortoise. A female tortoise came in last night to lay her eggs. She would have buried her eggs deep in the sand. An after weeks of incubation, the eggs will hatch. Eventually, cute little turtles will head for the ocean. Although, there is a high risk of predators eating them before they can survive this period of incubation. Humans are one of these predators.

I continue my early morning walk, and think about surfing in Lower Baja many years earlier. Ah, 'many moons' have come and gone.

The Baja men would bring their fish on to the beach after returning from hours upon the ocean. The afternoon would be 'a buzz' with each boat's haul of fish. My surf buddies and I would assist the men with hauling their boats up the beach. It was then that we would talk over the price of purchasing a fish or two. Really, not much haggling went on, as one could usually buy a fish the size of your arm for twenty-five cents! Times and prices have changed since my early surf trips so long ago.

One such afternoon, a large tortoise is brought in within the day's catch. This tortoise is really a majestic creature, just beautiful. Though, within a few moments, one of the local men turns the tortoise over, and stabs it in the heart with his knife!

I'm wide-eyed, and not sure of what is going down. This display of cultural diversity is different than anything I have seen before. Next, the man gets his mouth over the opening he created in the tortoise, and sucks the blood out! (A local boy y tells us the blood of the tortoise's heart is an aphrodisiac). After a long moment, the fisherman looks up from his feasting with a huge bloody grin. Apparently he feels his machismo will be in full glory tonight.

I'm always amazed at the different habits each culture brings to our world. The heart of a tortoise certainly isn't my cup of tea, but I understand there are ethnic diversities everywhere. Here in Baja, this is how life is lived.

LET US BE FOREVER

If macaws mate for life, what happens when one partner dies? Does the surviving macaw feel sadness, or is there no feeling? What happens to the survivor?

We were together for twenty years, or was it thirty? There was always perfection of how we nurtured each other. Because of our love, there was nothing more that we needed in our world.

One summer day you became very tired. You told me you were exhausted, too tired to fly anymore. I thought it was because of our early morning hunt. I did not concern myself until you started to lower your head, and you had a hard time breathing.

I nursed you for days. I would urgently fly off for whatever was necessary, only to return and find you even more drained. Your eyes began to become glazed. There was a faraway look behind them. I tried to act as if today was just like any other day in our lives. I was trying to keep you in this world. I told you that tomorrow you would be healthy, although we both knew this would never be. I would keep saying that all would soon be better. I think I did this to protect myself because my heart was breaking.

You wanted me to hold you closer. You quietly whispered, "even closer." I covered you with my wings. I wanted to protect you from everything that was taking you away, but I couldn't stop the universe from unfolding. I would tell you how your feathers, with their deep colors, were so beautiful. They were just as magnificent as the day we first met, so long ago. You leaned against my chest. I knew that all I could do in these last few days was make you as comfortable as possible. I tried to be brave and strong, but I was crying. I didn't want you to go away.

Others would pass by, but they didn't stop. They sensed that we were supposed to be alone. The atmosphere of the jungle had a feeling of sadness. The air was so very still. The brilliant sunrise and sunset still kept us company, but I became desperate to see the sun each day, knowing that these were your last days of warmth.

In your final hour, you were in another place. You occasionally turned to me, your far away eyes telling me it is all right. Everything is all right. I watched your last few breaths. You became more peaceful in those last moments.

And then it was over, or does it start?

I sat for a long, long time. There was nothing to announce to the world. I just tried to accept that you were not in my life. You were still here near me, but not of this world anymore. There you lay, colorful feathers, and all that life meant to me.

I scattered some of those loving feathers over the jungle. This is where our lives had been absorbed, so it felt appropriate. For the first few days I continued with my normal routine of gathering food, but I had no appetite. I sat for two days and did not eat. I only thought of you. One night, I imagined I heard you telling me not to be sad. I became silent and considered never speaking again. I didn't know what was going on in my head. I didn't understand those feelings.

One morning, at sunrise, I flew off toward the deep part of the jungle. I just felt that I needed to fly. It felt good to become one with the sky. On that day, I was soaring! I thought that if the hawks saw me now, they would think that I was one of them. I wanted to be something different than what I was. I felt that I became a different creature, and kept flying. I eventually came to rest in the large branches of an old balsa tree. Other birds stopped to look at me, but we didn't speak, I know they sensed my distant spirit. This balsa tree became my resting place for a week. Many times, I would think of our favorite tree, and imagine you there, waiting for me.

Today, I am flying deeper into the canopy, deeper into the vast emerald hue. This new world, lands that are not familiar, helps me forget that my heart and life feel so lonely, so empty. As I glide above a forest that is scented with a tear, I realize that my thoughts of the life we shared together are not as constant as they were when you first left me behind. I feel guilty for not thinking of you all the time. Somewhere inside I know this is all part of my healing.

My journey here on the earth is not yet over, but I wish it were.

For now, I must continue to fly. I am flying on, forever.

There Was a Woman

there was a woman
she looked just like you
I couldn't stop myself
memories of you came flooding back into my mind

the woman had your same mouth
those same cheekbones
the wavy auburn hair
that slender waist
the perfect hips
she had that sweet, sensual look that you carried with you
that look that easily held me captive

so often, you would throw yourself into my arms
always, with lustful eyes and warm lips
we colored our time together with comfort and trust
we gathered strength from each other
you and I were addicted to our romance
all that loving that filled our lives
all that caring and happiness
you were the heartbeat of my life

today's afternoon sun slowly invades this house
I can still feel your presence here
I can sense your shadow slowly moving across the walls
and after so long a time, your lovely scent still remains

distant steps of my memory
you are gone, but you linger
you slowly pace through my life

it was easy to say goodbye
only moments
thoughtful and protective

I rid myself of you
familiar things began to disappear
new towels lined the shelves

new sheets covered the bed

these new habits helped and yet, months later
a vision of you dropping your towel to the floor
with a pleasing smile and a sigh

when I am alone, and the afternoon sun warms my face
I dream
I remember trying to catch my breath from loving so hard
our romance was a river of magic

swept away in that river
romance lost
we betrayed each other
we betrayed our souls
you lost yourself in other men
you were searching for the love that had once kept us in paradise
I turned to other women
bodies I wasn't accustomed too
it helped, but I was so lonely for you
I always wanted to be somewhere else
a place full of love, with someone that understood my spirit
someone like you

that woman that reminded me of you
it took my breath away
I don't want to reminisce
it hurts too much

distant lover

my lost friend
I need to see this brilliance again
I need to feel love's wild intoxication once more
I will open my heart, and discover what true love can do to my life
I must

AMERICA

I received an email today from Italy. My beautiful lady friend can't wait till we see each other again. It is nice to know she has been thinking about me. I have a good feeling about this woman. I 've been sending her some new poetry that I've been composing, and they are full of love and lust.

I'm tickled that such an attractive woman is looking forward to my arrival in Italy. Maybe what we shared here in the tropics was just what she needed in her life? We did have a chemistry that fit very well together, and that was an impressive week we spent romancing one another. We were happily caught up in the thrill of new and wild pleasure!

There'ss a visiting American woman in town, and she seems to be trying to get to know me better. She has been dropping subtle hints. I do admit that she does looks sexy strollong the shoreline. But, I think she's really not my type—whatever that might be.

The author, Nikos Kazantzakis soulfully wrote in his novel, *Zorba the Greek*, that Zorba felt it was a sin to let any woman sleep alone. Ah, lots of praise for women in that book. Adhering to Zorba's philosophy, I would usually be ready to explore any possibility with the American beauty,, but with the email from Italy, I am doing my best to ward off the American's attempts. Although I do admit, she is very inviting.

The woman (throwing the subtle hints) catches up to me after surfing and invites me to meet her at the café later this evening.Gosh, I really don't have any excuses to give her for not meeting her later. I think that maybe I just won't show up, that should give her a message. Maybe, l won't well this evening? Who knows, maybe I will show up for the date, and just be sociable. Talking is fine with me.

I don't go to the café at the hour dictated. I stay home at my cottag, and stay busy with editing the new manuscript. Hopefully, she will understand that I am not interested.

Suddenly there is a knock on my front door! I know it has to be her.

I greet her warmly, invite her inside, and offer her something to drink. Though, I think she's already been drinking.

The first thing she asks is why I didn't show up at the café. I rattle off a couple of lame excuses, and feel embarrassed. I really don't want to hurt her feelings, so I sort of level with her. With some flattery, I say that I 'd usually be in hot pursuit of a woman that is so sexy, but I have been involved with another woman. Half true!

The statement works well for a moment. That was easy! Then, to my surprise, the young woman stands up, and pulls her dress straight off! Just like that! I mean we didn't even kiss first! She's not wearing a bra, and I really can't say those are underpants! Jeez, that's a very sexy piece of silk!

So, there I sit, and this tanned, sensuous body rests a few inches from my mouth, and no real excuses to spit out. So, what the hell, I dive in—hook, line and sinker. With women and beauty, I have no willpower at all. I figure it is like going surfing. Sitting in the ocean is nice, but the real thrill of surfing is paddling into the wave, and riding it! And if you are going to take off on a wave, commit yourself, ride it with style! She welcomes me with all she has, and sparks fly!

Our time together is very hot, and I am glad we indulged in so much spice. She and I know this does not mean much, it is just sex, and it's great sex.

She's happy and curls up against my chest, my arm around her shoulder. We lay like this for a short time, and I think she is falling asleep. The feeling now comes over me that I wish I were alone. I just want to go to sleep by myself. I know this is selfish, rude, chauvinistic, not cool, but remember, I wasn't into this; she is just not my type. If I were at her house, I would just kiss her goodnight, excuse myself, and skip home. But I realize that she will be staying the night.

I get up, brush my teeth, throw some water on my face, and head back to bed. I know it's not so terrible and things could be worse. Resigned to my fate, I try to fall asleep. Everybody understands the perimeters of their own comfort zone, so this is just about my comfort zone.

The next morning, I am up early and busy around the cottage. She sleeps in! This is getting to me! I want my space! She finally wakes and is ready for more of last night's fireworks. But I think…just get dressed and get out of here. That was fun, but can't you see I am ready to move on with the day and you are not part of it.

She senses my attitude and starts to pout. Fine, I don't care; pout all you want. She asks if she can take a shower. Sure, I say. I feel bad about not even giving her a *good morning kiss*, but maybe she is on her way.

She does her best to stretch her sexy legs as she gets off the bed. She then leaves the bathroom door ajar so she can expose her beautiful bottom as she bends over to start the shower. Jeez! Come on, I may be mean and insensitive, but I am a man! And that derriere of yours is the most beautiful thing I have seen in a long time, at least since last night! Oh, what the hell!

I enter the bathroom, don't say a thing, and just let her carry on. She finally smiles, grabs my hand and walks me into the shower. With my shorts and t-shirt soaked, she slowly undresses me. We turn an uncomfortable morning into a class on "how to make a shower feel like a million bucks."

Like Zorba, I know women need to be nurtured, and they need to be loved. A woman needs to feel like a woman! They deserve to have the best sex possible. We live in a world that is full of uncertainty, and maybe good lovemaking is a simple way to tell the world to fuck off! We are going to have fun and I am sorry if someone's feelings may get hurt someday. Today, let's take it into the fire, and fly to heaven!

SUMMER FIRE

summer kiss the night
sky blanket
    deep blue
        to black

the long night
sharing
    exploring you
        loving you

naked
your arms
    your long fingers
stretched
    in poetic pose

tonight
I've been
    everywhere
        within your body and soul
I feel saturated with
    the pure woman that you are

wrapped in each other's arms
our growing warmth
a world of smoldering desires
this heat could start a forest fire

stretching for miles
    uncontainable
        inexhaustible
heaven and hell all in flames

we did not want to stop
our senses
    burned to the ground
        to the earth
            to the beginning

Balsawood Surfboard

I share a delicious dinner with my neighbors last night. I also enjoye our after dinner conversation. There, on the porch, we start to 'talking story' with a couple of bros about surfing.

Somewhere in the mix about surfboards and shapers, I say that I've wanted a balsawood surfboard shaped by Dick Brewer. (Dick is a legendary surfer/shaper of the early days of surfing. Throughout the years, he has set the standard for many shapers on board design, and he still shapes beautiful boards today).

Living in Central America for the winter, and being so close to South America, I I should travel into the jungles of Ecuador and find the balsawood necessary to create a surfboard blank. Eventually, a shaper like Brewer will cut it to my, and their, specifications.

The image sent one of my companions off to narrating a marvelous story. I was transfixed as he painted a wonderful tale of hiking deep into the jungle of Ecuador, meeting a shaman, finding the perfect balsa tree neded for the task of making the surfboard.

All of us became fascinated and lost in our friend's colorful imagery. His eyes were bright with enchantment! If he were transported back, many years, to my college story telling class, he'd have gotten an A+ for his presentation!

Occasionally, one of us would bring up our take on what might happen next in his story. This additional 'food' just sent our storyteller off with more wonder and imagination. He wove an amazing visual that we all loved. His tall tale was my evening's highlight.

Perhaps, I will some day be in that jungle, and have a perfect balsawood tree speak to me in the language of my own heart. And, my adventure will make for grand words and imagery. Though, my friend's story on a warm night in the tropics is embedded into my mind forever. That's the power of poetically crafting a good yarn.

The American Dream

I spend a few nights with Miss America before her departure back to the States. I don't know how well she would do in the singing and dancing segment of the *real* Miss America Pageant, but she would score exceptionally well in the swimsuit competition!

We have a good time, and with no strings attached. We're bedroom buddies. We are just enjoying each other as lovers. And it's been a tremendously sweet relationship!

I slept at her house last night. She likes those circular designs adorned with yarn, feathers and beads that are crafted to catch one's dreams, a *'Dream-Catcher'*.

DREAM-CATCHER

you keep a Dream-Catcher in your window
I gaze at the colorful yarn of its geometric shape
    centuries of dreams
you said it works
    you dreamed me

once, your dreams were full of gallant men and sinful women
    many nights you were caressed and loved by them all
seductive twilight of the growing moon, I came to you in a deep dream
    I was a king dressed in velvet
        you were an empress in silk
            we danced in the clouds
then we were naked
    and I carried you to your bed

an early morning sun warms your bedroom
    subtle colors spread against the walls
a slight breeze blows through an open window
the Dream-Catcher slowly twists in the wind
    I can see both sides of the dream

our love is like a dream
we time travel through it
    not quite awake
        catching a good night's sleep in between dreams

SAILING INTO THE SUNSET

Since my discovery of Point Carlota, I've returned a few times, and have scored good waves each trip. The family is always happy to see me, so my frequenting the banana farm is a wonderful experience. Although I'd like to take some photos and have them plastered all over the walls of my cottage, I have kept the surf a secret. I know, in time, other surfers will stumble onto the great waves of the point. I also know that I was probably not the first person to surf the place. Though, it is fun to make believe.

This return is a bit different, as a sailboat has anchored off the point. My first thoughts are of disappointment, but since meeting the boatowners, I have come to realize it all as a blessing.

The Black Empress is a beautiful, sleek catamaran with stunning design. It has all the modern equipment and ample space for any voyage. The boat was so named for her graceful black hull that easily slips through the sea with amazing speed and smoothness. Perhaps, the boat was also named after the beautiful black empresses that live throughout the islands of the Caribbean.

Point Carlota is certainly off the radar screen for most surfers, so sharing waves with this couple is a welcome change. I'd always rather share waves with fun-loving folks than surf alone.

Over dinner and drinks one night we become good friends. The family grows! After a couple days of surfing together, they ask me if I would like to crew with them for a couple of weeks. They promise the discovery of some great coves for anchoring, eating fresh lobster and fish, snorkeling in crystal clear water, and riding a few uncharted reefs. These colorful scenarios are all my favorite side of sailing!

Though, I'm not *wild* about sailing, I concede to their pictures of grandeur and tell them to count me in. As I mentioned, being anchored in a serene bay and diving into warm water in the morning is very pleasant. It is everything else which goes along with sailing that can be a struggle: It's the constant adjustment of the sails, the heavy weather that can spring up out of nowhere, and the beating your body goes through in rough seas, all these things take away from those limited tranquil hours. Truthfully, over the years, my surfboard is my most comfortable vessel for ocean excursions.

We are to meet back at my cottage in a few days, and then we are supposed to sail away for a couple of weeks.

I return home after my visit to Point Carlota. It's always good to return to the serenity of my simple cottage. I'm planning on this sailing voyage, but I'm not sure this is what I really want to do with my time. I like my life without getting on a sailboat and breezing into the ocean depths. I enjoy my fresh orange juice in the early morning. I love the surf that I ride, and my beach. I know I need new adventures like sailing, so...I decide to sleep on it. I feel the right decision will unfold. It usually does.

A few days later the Black Empress sails into the bay off of the peninsula. My new friends are happy to eat the excellent cuisine at the café, and they easily fall into the lifestyle of the town. They understand why I like my space and time around here, and why I have become a little apprehensive about my agreement to go sailing.

One evening, try to back out of sailing with them for the two-week adventure. I explain that I am reluctant about the voyage. I will be spending my time thinking about my cottage and the palm trees, the waves, and my life here on this quiet coast.

They are disappointed, almost offended. The conversation goes on throughout the evening, and before the end of the night (and a couple of bottles of wine), I have again agreed to go along with our original plans of sailing together for a couple of weeks. *This decision to accompany them will soon come back to haunt me as our trip is full of mishap...this misfortune unfolds to eventually confirm my foreboding!*

I should know better than to agree with something that just doesn't feel correct. If it didn't feel comfortable, I should've let it go. I decided long ago that sojourns through life should not have any apprehension attached to them. I understand that life is not so cut and dry, but if my angels are looking out for me (which they usually are) I can live with a clear conscious and sleep in peace. So against my better judgment, I set off on an exciting and perilous journey!

SHARK

My God! It must be midnight, and this boat is flying! A blinding rain is making it difficult to do anything. The breeze is getting stronger and it is now necessary to change the sails! This is the world of sailing and one has to take care of the business-at-hand. Because it's so damn dark tonight, it feels like we are travelling at some super-sonic speed! There are no rules out here; just nature, survival, and it's one hell of a rush…

Life aboard a boat…
A sailboat can make a good home, a moving home. And the thrill of sailing can be spectacular! The wind can blow a sailor from one island to another. Making for a great life.

The world has so many islands to venture toward, and many folks love to daydream about the life of owning a boat, and living the adventure!

There are a series of beautiful islands that spot this coast, and the white beaches of these islands are spectacular! Throw in the perfect clear water and you have your dream completed. Those that sail, cherish the sacred breeze.

I have been reluctant to go sailing with my new friends, yet I know the adventure will be good for my spirit. Though this adventure has been nicely presented, I still have apprehension as I board for a two-week cruise.

Anybody who has spent time on the ocean knows that wind, adrenaline, awareness and caution all go hand in hand. I have written about the comfort of anchoring in a clear, warm cove. And, I've also written about the other side of sailing, the side that takes one away from that comfort zone.

Well here I go, off sailing. It will be necessary to stay alert, batten down the hatches and stow the gear as I sail off into the unknown…

It's a warm breeze that keeps us on a fast run on the leeward side of this group of islands. The Black Empress, the catamaran, is 'on the wind" or 'close-hauled', and really flying over the ocean. This is an amazing vessel, and it cost a lot of money. The money doesn't seem to be a problem with the owners. They aren't flamboyant with their lifestyle, yet they are happy to spend money to keep everything shipshape aboard the Black Empress.

The owners, a husband and wife team, are good surfers and they like to stop at any quality reef for a few hours of surfing. This is fine with me, because if we spot any good waves, we drop anchor, go for a surf. My kind of people!

I'm not sure how the owners make their living, and I feel it is not my business to ask. I respect a *tight lip* about how we all get by, and I am a bit annoyed when someone presses me about my life and how I survive.

Life aboard a sailing vessel can keep you busy. There certainly are times when the steady breeze has everybody relaxed and enjoying *the sail*. And, there are times when the crew is in the full 'business mode'. The fine-tuning of the sails, halyards, lines, the piloting, the navigation, the food preparation, and anything else that arises, simply has to be taken care of, and taken care of immediately.

Sailing at night is usually *four-hours-on, four-hours-off*. Everybody has a scheduled time of being on duty. We've been a well-tuned team for this first week of sailing. The owners have an itinerary of seeing specific islands, and we are spending a good deal of time understanding the boat and each other. We've been getting a few waves on some offshore reefs, so we also have the surf 'buzz' going. After this trip is over and done with, even if it will be years, I sense we will always stay friends. That's the nice thing about life; the 'tribe' keeps getting bigger.

Trouble on the horizon…

The sun set a couple of hours ago when suddenly the wind shifts! And at that moment, the air has become very still. The evening sky is becoming blacker. We are all on deck thinking about our next plan of action when the owner states that we should batten down everything that needs to be secure, and be alert to handle whatever chores may be necessary if asked.

The storm hits us fast and hard! We don't have any time to reef the main sail, or replace the front headsail. We don't have time for lifelines, or life vests, or much else! The wind, rain and ocean just unleash an enormous amount of fury in the blink of an eye!

It is getting rougher out here, and heavier seas are accompanying the storm. The boat suddenly jolts, and turns on one pontoon. We are on one hull and losing control! The husband is screaming at the top of his lungs for his wife's attention, as a few seconds earlier she had jumped below to secure everything possible. He senses trouble, and struggles to leave the helm to get to his wife. I take over steering the boat as best as possible.

He goes below just in time to see his wife knocked off balance and thrown backwards. Her head smacks into a bulkhead, and she becomes unconscious. I'm doing my best at the helm, trying to steer the boat in some manner. I move away from the wind, and let the sails loosen. Because of the storm's intensity, there is no controlling the situation. The boat looking like one of those plastic toys in the bathtub—just before a three-year-old child takes it down!

Things aren't good and they aren't getting any better! As the storm rages, a few lines start to snap. The boat is now making strange sounds, and I think the mast will be coming down next. Because the wind and rain are making so much noise, it is almost impossible to communicate with the others. Isee the owner look out at me from the cabin, but he's soon gone as his attention is on his wife.!

Different parts of the boat are popping and snapping apart. Bolts, cleats, wood, fiberglass start flying. These objects are being projected everywhere and with velocity! I duck down and cover my head as two such boat lines swish by me. Soon, another line is against my back, and its tension moves me a few feet before I hear "twang," and the line snaps. I am doing whatever I can to save myself, and lie as flat as possible so not to be hit by one of those flying booby traps.

Something shoots out of nowhere and strikes me right in my back! I can feel a shooting pain in between my shoulder blades. I am now in the boat's cockpit, covering and protecting my head from the flying debris!

As the mast comes falls, it brings even more of the deck hardware and lines with it! The two hulls that kept us fairly stable thirty minutes ago, are now default. One may be taking on water, because we aren't at all upright.

The horror of the storm continues for another five minutes, and suddenly, as fast and as hard as it has hit us, it then disappears! The Gods must have had a terrible argument up in the heavens because that is the most vicious display of nature I have ever seen! The sky is now clear, and the stars shine. The thunderous noise that had previously filled the night's air has disappeared, and now, there's stillness about us.

My back aches from where I was struck, but I feel okay. I'm fortunate that my skull wasn't smashed!. The owners don't emerge from below, so I rush over to see what's happening. I find the owner with his wife in his arms. She *coming around,* and getting her consciousness back. She's crying. Her husband console her, whispering that the storm has passed.

I make my way back on deck and inspect the damage. The owner and his wife soon follow. No one says anything substantial for quite awhile. We are all trying to get our bearings back after such an explosion of nature. We realize our misfortune of being in the middle of such a storm front. We are lucky that we weren't thrown overboard. The storm has passed, but we are far from being out of trouble. Without any words, we start looking over the vessel, and after a few minutes of surveying the situation, we gather together and discuss the damage.

It looks like the mast and all lines are in no usable condition. The radio is inoperable, and communication with the outside world is void. Other necessary equipment was shattered or got excessively wet from salt water. You would think a two-way radio would be available, but not so. We discover that much of the food is not salvageable. We do have enough drinkable water for a few days, and some canned goods to eat. The fact that both engines cannot start is a major dilemma. The other serious problem is that one of the two hulls is slowly taking on water. The two hulls stayed intact, but the stress of the storm damaged the side of the starboard hull.

We take a couple of hours to sort through all the debris, and eventually discuss our next step in getting the boat into port.

I shake my head about the foreboding feeling I had of making this voyage. I was apprehensive even coming aboard in the first place, it just didn't feel right! I should have listened to my *inner voice*. I also understand that there is absolutely no sense in dwelling on that now. I just shake my head in disbelief. Apparently, I was supposed to be here for a reason. I'm not sure why, but maybe I was meant to be here as a trusted companion. I shrug my shoulders and laugh a little about our predicament.

My smile is a welcome sight to the owners, and they become as positive as possible. We'll be Okay.

Surprisingly, my surfboard was in the one hull that stayed intact, and the board isn't damaged. I suggest that I paddle my surfboard to the nearest island and secure a boat to tow us back to safety. I'm ready to do whatever is necessary. But, though we can see an island in the distance, the skipper isn't comfortable with my paddling in open ocean. He feels the chance of my not making it to land safely would be much worse then losing his sailboat!

The following morning we attempt to rig for wind power by constructing a makeshift mast and boom that sailcloth can be attached. Our trouble is that one hull is half submerged, and is working as an anchor. The newly renovated sail and mast won't do us much good. Although the effort is exhausting, we do get rigged for wind power. Though, I don't think it's enough to make headway.

I again suggest my paddling for help. The owner understands, but doesn't want me to leave yet. Maybe a fishing boat will pass nearby today?

At sunset, we make it through a sparse dinner of canned peaches and some crackers. One bottle of Kahlua was found undamaged, so the three of us sip on that. The wife's head is going to be all right, although she has a good bump. There isn't much dry room to sleep down below, so up top, aboard the deck, is the best spot to curl up and try to get some rest. One of us stays awake for a few hours to watch for any lights out on the horizon.

The next morning things seem to be getting worse. Our enthusiasm for being rescued is waning.

The owner seeks me out, and tells me to do my best with paddling for help. I understand his decision to not let me leave earlier, and I'm glad he's now agreeing for my departure.

I salvage through the pontoon to secure my surfboard. It has a quality board bag (the kind one uses for airline flights) protecting it throughout the fury of the storm, so it's not damaged. I find my small backpack that contained my passport and some cash. So not to get soaked, and ruined, I always keep both, passport and cash, in a plastic case they stay dry. I find a hat to utilize for protection from the sun. I sure hope I can paddle the distance without any misfortune...I don't want to have to swim for it!

The owner gives me a liter of water and shakes my hand. He tells me their plan is to keep the makeshift sail aloft. If another storm hits them, he'll drop the anchor to try and attempt to keep from drifting away.

The distant island is probably farther away than we suspect, but it's a good day for a paddle. I sit on top of my trusty 7'6" surfboard. It is a thick board, made for big waves, and it's a decent board for paddling. It's not a streamlined, 16' paddleboards with a lot of speed, but today, this board I'm upon! This surfboard has been my pride and joy on countless waves. It's always been dependable, and it has to be dependable now.

I am off, and about hundred yards from the boat. I turn back and take a look. I signal acknowledgement, and they wave back. I have to do my best and get those folks rescued.

It feels good to be aboard my surfboard and be moving through the water. Helplessly sitting aboard the boat was frustrating, so I'm happy to be on the ocean and making the effort for land. It also feels so good to stretch the muscles.

An hour later, and I'm a small speck on a large sea. The island to which I am heading really doesn't appear any closer to me from when I first started, but I know I am moving in the right direction. I think of the great Hawaiian waterman, Eddie Aikua, and how he was never heard of again after paddling his surfboard for help in much the same circumstance as my own. Eddie's spirit lives on! In my mind, there is no way I won't make it to land! I wonder if Eddie felt the same way? I am sure he did, but that's not my issue, I am on my way to this island, and all will be fine.

After three hours of stroking, I'm worn out. I stop every so often and drift. I occasionally sit upright so my back can get some relief from the strain of this workout. Although I often switch from paddling flat, or prone, on my tummy to knee paddling, my back is getting a workout! I know I am going deep into my endurance core to keep paddling. These moments of fatigue usually end as fast as they arrive, and I just put my head down, and continue.

An hour later, and the island is growing in size as I approach. I can see two large volcanic peaks, and the island's interior is brilliant green. This is encouraging, and I stroke a little harder. That only lasts for five or ten minutes, before I rest again. I am extremely thirsty. I tried to kold off drinking water for as long as possible, but I finished that liter a long ago. I can't believe I once had ambitions to be a long distance paddler. At this moment, that seems so far away from any desire that I can muster. Just give me a wave, a beach, and a pretty lady to enjoy the day! These thoughts sound grand, and I begin to daydream of beaches and women as I paddle.

Funny, how the simplest of things can relieve our tortures. The mind, and where you let it drift, is the biggest factor in any intense situation. I do understand that the conditioning of the mind is just as important as any other muscle in the body. Physical conditioning for marathoners is a must, but mental conditioning is just as important. It can be a battle just to complete in an event if you let your mind get the best of you. Most athletes understand their limit, but when they see the finish line in striking distance, they push themselves beyond that limit. It's human nature.

I am almost to my limit, and I'm nowhere near my finish line! I must keep going.!I have to stay focused! I have to make it! That's always been my attitude with any endeavor. I can't see any other way to look at life. Just put your head down and paddle!

I haven't spotted any other watercraft on the ocean, but if I did, they probably havinf a difficult seeing me within the sun's blinding glare. I don't have any flares to signal a boat. We lit a few flares from the boat on the first night following the storm. And, the flares that were left aboard, will be used when the owner sees fit.

I'm so exhausted...I am not sure if I can see straight. I feel like I'm having an *out-of-body* experience. I just need to drift for a short time, and rest.

I realize that I have fallen asleep. Losing my balance is why I wake. I shake myself back to reality, steady the board and begin paddling again. Off to my right I spot a fin. It's about 100 yards away. The shark is swimming along with me, and obviously, checking me out.

I know that fear is the worst thing that I need right now! I'm not happy to see this creature appear, but I have nothing against this shark. This attituse sounds foolish to most people, but 'the shark spirit' has been passed on through tales and songs for hundreds of years in many South Sea cultures. I've read stories about Polynesians swimming alongside sharks, making eye contact, and having the shark accompany them as a guide, a *spirit gude.*

So, I continue to paddle, and keep an eye on this massive creature. I think to myself that the film, "Jaws," made so many decades ago, can still keep people out of the ocean. That's the power of movies and the stories they weave. How many times have I heard someone say, "How can you go in the ocean? There are sharks out there"! In the amount of time that it took me to write this statement, there have been thousands of devastating auto accidents, and probably not one shark attack!

The automobile is a million times more dangerous than a shark! Don't take me wrong. I fully understand that the people that have been attacked by a shark, or have witnessed an attack, say that it is absolutely terrible! I've been told, it's like a seeing a dinosaur rise from the depths! It is horrifying! I can't imagine! Enough said! I don't take a shark attack lightly! I just don't want to dwell on it right now!

Here I am sounding brave and naïve about trusting that nothing will happen to me. Funny, what if he swims over, and tries to take a bite out of me!

Thank goodness there are no problems, and the shark disappears below the surface. I'll stay aware of his presence, and check often to see if he returns.

Within thirty minutes of the shark's disappearance more fins surface. Though, I rest easy because these are the dorsal fins of dolphins. The appearance of dolphins is a grand sight for all surfers and sailors! Their presence always changes the atmosphere of Neptune's Garden. Dolphins are fast, intelligent, playful, friendly, and are an addition to one's spirit. I've had the opportunity to surf alongside them many times. They surf with pure grace and power! The thrill of seeing these mammals ride the surf…coming toward you, flying in and through the waves, projecting into the air…it's something everybody should experience!

The presence of so many dolphin has added stamina to my strokes, and I have a new enthusiasm for reaching my destination! The island is getting much closer! It looms big and beautiful a couple of miles away! If I can keep up my pace, I could be there in an hour. I'm too far out to sea to make out any beaches or towns, but I have conviction that I will eventually arrive. I never felt that I wasn't going to make it to shore. I just let my mind give me every excuse to feel pain. How are my friends doing back on the boat? I hope they are holding up okay. I wish I weren't so tired!

Another thirty minutes, I am making better time than suspected. I see the island is a large mass of jungle vines, palm trees, and white beaches. I don't see any vessels or towns yet, but I head toward the closest beach. Hopefully there is a road that circles the island, bringing all the island's inhabitants together. There's got to be people, a main town, a harbor and some fishing boats. If I can find a road and get around this island, so to secure a boat for the rescue.

I am close now, and the shore looks so inviting. I am happy there is no reef, or heavy shore break that will hinder my getting off the ocean. I am so tired. I'm not sure I can paddle much longer.

I finally see sand under my surfboard as I stroke the last fifty yards! What a great sight those textured lines of sand are! Eventually, I'm in shallow enough water to slide off my board and walk on the sea's sandy bottom. The earth never felt so good!

When I reach the beach I drop my surfboard and collapse in the sand! I lie here for five minutes, half unconscious, half aware of my arrival on the island. I roll over on to my back, and I feel how sore my muscles have become. I also discover that I'm badly sunburned.

I sit up and survey the scene. Not a fucking soul anywhere! Just void of all life in every direction. I must be on the other side of the island's cultural center. You know, there must be one of the colorful outposts with the pastel colored homes and red tile roofs, fruit stands, and a hip bistro!

After a brief rest, I make haste through the jungle to see if there is an available coast road. I'm very thirsty and I wish I had some fresh water to drink. I am also terribly tired, and I can hardly carry my surfboard. I have to grab one end and drag the board across the sand. Within minutes, the board gets too much for me to hold, and I have to toss it to the side. I wanted to keep the board in case there is no road, and I have to paddle around a headland. I leave it, and hope to again locate in the future.

A few hundred yards later, I do stumble on a small road. I turn north, and hope this is the direction of the closest village. After an hour of walking, the road curves down to a home along the ocean's shore. The inhabitants spot me as I approach and aren't alarmed. They're thinking that I am just another tourist whose car broke down while circling their island.

I approach them and communicate the urgency of my predicament. I am very animated with my speech and arms explaining to them about the boat, the crew, and how I got here! The family gets wind of the seriousness of the situation, and I'm told that they will drive me to the office of the Harbormaster.

Happily, I climb into the man's truck, and he hits the gas pedal. And, hits it, he does! We are driving around every corner with abandonment, totally flying! This haste is fine with me, as I just want to get a search party together as soon as possible.

Eventually, we arrive at a port where small fishing boats line the shore. Larger fishing vessels are scattered along a dock. I scan the dock, and see a skipper and his crew aboard a large vessel. I jump out of the truck and approach the powerboat. I have great luck as the captain speaks English, and understands the urgency of the rescue. He quickly jumps into action with his boat and crew.

The captain turns a key, does some minor adjustments of throttle and we are off, and quickly out of the harbor, and traveling in the direction of the boat's location. Night is starting to fall, and the boat's location may be difficult to navigate to, but we have to try. Although I am fatigued and my body is working on *overtime*, my adrenaline is pumping. I've been drinking water nonstop, and the crew has fixed some food for me to eat, so I'm alert enough to keep going.

As we race out to sea, I think how fortunate to have made my long paddle in the daylight, and not within the a darkness of night!

I can't believe how fast we are traveling and how much distance we've traveled in such a short time! The same distance I paddled for the entire day is only taking a couple of hours tonight on this boat!

We eventually near the vicinity of where I think the boat may have drifted. We turn off the engines and try to listen for any sounds as to acknowledge the sailboat's whereabouts. There is no moon to shed any light on the ocean, and the night is dark!

We don't see them anywhere! We figure they may have drifted north, so we restart the engines, and hope we are correct in our calculations. They could have drifted anywhere!

We travel a few miles further, and through the darkness, we think there may be something out there—perhaps the boat? We go a short distance, and again shut the engines down. No sooner than we do, and we hear some shouts that are fairly close. Then a flare goes off about 200 yards away, and marks their spot. I am glad the owner saved that flare for when he thought necessary.

As we get closer, cheers light up the evening from both their boat and ours. The powerboat's strong lamp puts enough light on the sailboat to see both husband and wife waving and shouting for joy! The captain of the rescue boat is on his two-way radio giving the details of the sailboat to port authorities. The rescue boat's crew works quickly stabilizing the sailboat so my friends can board the powerboat. Once onboard, I get a big hug and sincere thank you.

When we finally get back into port, it is necessary to go to the local medical facility to check on our health. We are all okay, just worn out. After a few days of recuperating, we are all feeling physically better, and we start making our plans to return to our respected homes. I miss my cottage more than ever. I've been thinking of the Italian woman, and a few of the other wonderful ladies that have been part of my last few months. I am missing each every one of them, and have to smile with anticipation of what will unfold when I get back.

Sometime later, I received a note from my crew mates. They had a custom catamaran built and were cruising the Mediterranean. Ad later, I got a Christmas card, with a photo of their new baby. We kept in contact for a couple of years, and then our connection faded. Losing contact with friends happens, but I still consider these folks, family. We shared a life-threatening experience that made a huge impact on our lives, and we were all thankful to have lived through it.

By the way, I did return after the paddling fiasco, and retrieved my trusty surfboard. I also brought a bottle of expensive bottle of wine to share with the man that drove me into town that day after the paddle. We drank a glass or two.

My return to my home is a grand occasion. I'm so happy to get back to this cottage! I vow to myself that I won't go sailing for a long time! When I am finally settled, I grab a surfboard and walk straight down toward the ocean...

LET'S GET OUT OF HERE

Sometimes you feel like you have to get home! You have been sleeping on sandy beaches, sharing meals, campfires and laughs, and loving the beach life, but eventually there is a time when all involved decide that it's time to hit the road towards home. You've grown tired of the vagabond's life, and you are ready for a hot shower, full refrigerator, and everything that makes a home...a home. Sure, friends are one of life's greatest blessings, but having your own comfort zone and not sharing it 24/7 with them is certainly appreciated. It's just such a moment when my surf buddy and I looked at each other, and said, let's pack it up and drive home.

This journey was in an old Rambler. You may think that this isn't the best vehicle for the Baja desert, but it actually worked quite well! It wasn't the Rambler American, but it's design resembled a vintage Mercedes-Benz. It was a sweet ride, and it took me many miles till I eventually sold it.

My friend and I had driven the entire 1000-mile length of Baja. The desert point where we landed is not known for being a world-class surf destination, but no one else here, and that's what made it so appealing.

After a month, our food supply is wears thin, so we decide to leave for California. This entire trip's been a grand experience. We filled it with hours of surfing. But, it's time to head for greener pastures.

The Rambler started leaking odd engine fluids during the drive down, and it certainly didn't repair itself being parked by the tent. So, on our return trip, we check those trickling liquid levels often, and put in the appropriate amount of lubricant.

We seem to be making good time driving north, but somewhere out of Guerra Negro (a small semi-industrial town in the middle of Baja) the Rambler makes some odd noises, and stops running! We are caught in a dilemma as to what we should do. I own the car and it's not worth much money. It wouldn't be much of a loss, so I remark that I'm all for leaving the car where it sits. I say let's start grabbing what is necessary to carry, and find a bus somewhere. Considering the expense of towing and the time involved in trying to get this old car fixed, I just didn't think it would be worth all the effort to try and find a mechanic to repair it.

We sit and contemplate our next move, and at that moment, a truck pulls up behind the Rambler. It is an old Ford flatbed truck. These Ford trucks are quite a familiar sight on this highway. The truck's door flies open and a fellow steps out of the cab, followed by his young son. We talk to him in our limited use of Spanish, and then the man opens the Rambler's front hood and begins to survey the situation. I'm still in for leaving our stalled car, and just getting a ride with this fellow into the nearest town. Well, the man rolls up the sleeves of his white shirt, and jumps right in to fixing the car.

After a few minutes attempting to resolve the situation, he decides that a better, well-trained mechanic will have to fix the problem. He then moves his truck up in front of where the Rambler sits, and grabs a rope, and fastens his truck's rear bumper to our front bumper. He and his son climb into the truck; we climb into the Rambler, and off we go! And do we go! He starts flying! I mean he's hauling ass! I'd estimate 50mph! We are tied on about ten feet away from his truck, and are doing our best to watch for his brake lights to see if I have to apply the Rambler's brakes. I hope he has brake lights! This is a comedy and a hair-raising ride, but we end up enjoying the danger of the moment.

Our arrival at the mechanic's shop is met with no immediate emergency, just another gringo with a broken down car. The man that towed our vehicle to the mechanic has some business to attend too, and he and his son leave. Eventually the mechanic and two of his friends lean over the Rambler's engine and quietly talk about what has caused the trouble. My buddy and I grab our water bottles and wait for the verdict. We are both expecting to hear a sour conclusion about the car's condition, and are ready to grab all we can carry. Where is the bus station in this town? We relax in the shade of the mechanic's shop.

After a while, the three men start tearing into the engine, and soon, many of the engine's parts are strewn about. More discussion among them, and they tell us that there is a crack on the side of the fuel pump. I sigh, and figure the bus ride home will be our means of travel. We are told, and I already know, that ordering a new or used fuel pump for an old Rambler would take weeks to get here. I doubt they even make these anymore, and I opt for finding the bus again. Suddenly, the main mechanic is off with the broken car part without much word to anybody. His two friends go over and sit in the office. There really isn't much we can do, so I take out the cribbage board and cards, and we play a game. A few young kids that have been hanging around the shop drinking their Cokes are fascinated about the game and our *pegging* and the *laying down of our cards.*

An hour passes and the mechanic returns with a fuel pump that has now been welded together at one focal point. He's also fabricated a makeshift washer to make sure there is a tight seal. I utter the prevailing term of the era, "Unreal"!

All three men are involved with the instillation of the fuel pump and the assembling of the car parts. The mechanic turns the ignition, and the Rambler purrs like it is brand new! The engine sounds so sweet! My God, these guys are brilliant, what engineers! All three are proud of themselves for the achievement. I think they do this type of *backyard, seat of your pants* engineering everyday. These guys can fix anything!

So, I am wondering what all this will cost! Can you believe, five dollars later, my friend and I, in a very comfortable stylish Rambler that looks like a vintage Mercedes-Benz, are back on the highway!! The three mechanics wave at us, and then slowly head to the office to wait for the next question about automobiles, rocket science, or brain surgery. They didn't do us a favor for their financial benefit. They helped because it was in the spirit of knowing that someone needed their assistance. These guys just loved the challenge. Just another day at the office!

As we drive off, I spot the man that gave us the necessary tow to town. He and his son are parked at the hardware store, loading a few things into the back of his truck. I park the Rambler, and grab my surfboard that I've been traveling with here in Baja. With a big smile on my face, I offer the board to them. I say, as a sign of friendship, his son might enjoy having a surfboard. The young kid's eyes light up, and they graciously accept the gift. They thank me, and place the board in the back of his truck with the other supplies. We all shake hands, and my buddy and I drive off into the afternoon sun. Sometimes you just have to get home!

IRRESISTIBLE

This wild coast offers limitless possibilities for a traveling surfer. Some veterans of the road have suggested that they have seen it all, and there are just so many spots available for quality surfing. "Quality" has different meanings to different surfers. On this journey, I've discovered that there are countless bays, points, long sandy beaches, and *outer-islands* that hold many possibilities for great wave riding.

We are camping on a quiet beach, somewhere off the beaten track. The truck is filled with the essential staples like rice, peanut butter, onions and potatoes. We've been diving for fish, and there are some hidden convenient underwater rocks no more than forty yards offshore, so there are some good-sized fish available to catch. We've been spearing some beauties!

At high tide (tides here are radical on this coast, the ocean can have a twelve foot shift) we have been surfing a little point that is no more than five minutes from where we've been camping. There isn't much height to the waves because of this point being inside alarge bay. We've been having fun, and that's what is important. Of course, we always say that it would be unreal if it was two feet bigger. There isn't a surfer alive that hasn't uttered those words. We've been here throughout the growing, and full moon…it's been an excellent vacation.

This surfing excursion is with a woman who comes from Argentina. We've been been traveling together for a couple of months now. Besides style and charm, this woman is a striking beauty. I love that she is in great physical shape, she surfs, and that she can cook some amazing dishes. She can make the best meals out of the most simple and sparse ingredients. Her personality gets heated at times, and she can become a real firecracker! Luckily, this anger doesn't surface all that often. Most of the time her easy temperament seems to fit quite well with my simple approach to life. Her natural Spanish speaking skill has been a blessing for me as she is the designated 'team interpreter'. She is a very good companion, and a wonderful travel partner.

A local kid walked past our campsite earlier today. He was fishing with a hand-line, while walking down the coast. His little brother tagged along about ten yards behind. I'm sure his family was expecting some Dorado steaks to be cooked later this evening. The boy tells us that no more than one kilometer up the beach, right around the next bay, there are good waves. He goes on to say that the waves are much better, and bigger than where we are now camping. We know that one kilometer is probably five, but we decide that we will give it a try the following morning. This has been a comfortable beach to camp, but the call of surging surf rings loud and clear!

Daybreak finds the truck loaded with everything as secure as possible. This extra tightening of ropes and bungee cords is a necessity because the roads around here are all in terrible condition.

This all reminds me of a story one of my best friends once told me…

This friend is a "Baja veteran" and in the last forty years he's been hanging out in some of the most remote places he can find. All for the surfing, and the adventure!

So, one day, he's driving deeper and deeper into the bush. After a long day of four-wheeling to his desired destination, he finally turns the engine off. All this with a huge sigh of relief! He feels like quite the adventurer; another desperado, hidden from society. All this driving to get some virgin surf, and more "Baja" in his veins.

In the middle of the night, he hears a vehicle off in the distance. He stumbles out of his truck camper and spots headlights on the road he arrived on, and these headlights are coming his way. He thinks about how bad that road is, and how it rattled his big Dodge truck. His back is still a little tight from the all-day ride. When the car finally gets near him, he notes that it is an old Pinto wagon (remember when Ford made those?). The car, with a young mom driving, with her three young kids in the backseat, slows up enough to check out my friend. The mom waves hello, and floors it! And, the Pinto disappears into the night. She probably has to get home and get those kids to bed somewhere up the road.

My friend just smiles about all his 'machismo"'adventuring, and ponders the difference between his big, mean truck and the mother's Pinto. Humble Pie strikes again!

Back to my girlfriend and our adventure at the new camping spot…

The road ends is not as bad as we expected. Remember, these aren't real roads, nothing like American or European highways where billions of dollars are spent on construction and maintenance.

We eventually enter a large bay, and with the low tide, we four-wheel drive up the beach toward some white water we spot up at the far end of the bay. We haven't checked with binoculars yet, but it looks like there may be a wave up at that point that could be ridden. As we get closer to an out-cropping of rocks at the point, we notice another truck, with a large tent next to it. So we see someone else is camping where we are heading. We eventually find a nice level spot to park the truck, and far away from the *high-tide line*, and survey the area. We, of course, don't camp too close to the other truck as we respect their privacy, and our own. I'm sure they appreciate simple camping etiquette. I notice a couple of surfboards by the tent, so I imagine we'll see them in the ocean.

The waves are bigger than our previous surf camp, and the tides don't affect the surf as much. It's not the best-shaped wave in the world, but still lots of fun. Our new neighbors are two women from Oregon. They've been on this coast for a month. They have been learning how to surf, and they really like the privacy of this bay. Like us, these folks are just trying to escape the crowds.

For a couple of days we are all friendly with each other, yet still respecting our separate camp privacy. Most of our conversations are out in the line-up in between riding waves.

On the third evening, my girlfriend and I are sitting around the campfire, just grooving on everything. Our neighbors soon join us by the firelight. They've brought a bottle of Tequila with them and want to know if we want to share a little. That's 'right neighborly' of them.

Our evening is full of good conversation, laughs, and some surprises. I do notice that during our evening together of drinking, one of the women can't get her eyes off of my girlfriend. It becomes quite obvious that she's trying to get to know her better.

And later in the evening, after a good Tequila buzz, the neighbors look at each other, and then look at us, and then ask if we would like to spend the night with them. Wow! I didn't expect that! Well, golly gee, and all that!! I figured the two women were lovers, but this is a pleasant surprise, and quite an invitation. I actually expect my girlfriend to start making an excuse for us to not partake in the neighbor's lovely offer, but to my surprise, she just smiles, licks her lips, and turns to me for my consent. And I am certainly in favor of the offer! Yes ma'am, count me in, both of us!

What a night! Most people know that man's fantasy is to make love with two women, and to watch those two women make love to each other. As I enter the neighbor's tent, and the thought of sharing such intimacy with three women, well, I realize I am stepping into a den of delightful, combustible fervency!

Our neighbors have apparently been thinking about what my girlfriend looks like naked, because there is no stopping their focus and desire. They are giving me a lesson on all her vulnerable and stimulating body parts. I 've always been attentive to those erroneous zones, but watching it unfold in front of me, let's say, is very intriguing, and arousing! Thankfully, all three women include me in their excitement and pleasure. For a brief moment, I imagine myself as a gallant sheik enjoying the finer aspects of owning a harem.

This *bundle of loving* goes on for a few hours, and I am worn out—just *spent!* I thought I had enough an hour ago, but their persistent urging and moaning kept me in the fire. Happily, they had their way with me! And us!

I eventually escape the beehive of activity, and exhausted, I make it over to the back of the truck. I need something to eat! I smile, and imagine that if I were in America tonight, I would be opening the freezer door and pulling out a carton of Haagen-Dazs ice cream. But at this moment, it looks like canned peaches will be what I am devouring. Just what I need after burning so many calories back in the *den!*

My girlfriend joins me at the truck a few minutes later, and gets right into the feast. We don't say anything about what we've doing the last few hours. We just chomp away on the food.

We finally head for bed, and turn out the lights. With the covers drawn up around our necks, my 'Firecracker' whispers that she didn't surprise me too much, and that this evening of *wild sex* won't effect our being a couple. I kiss her cheek and tell her I love surprises, especially surprises like that!

It's an interesting few days on our beach. Our daylight hours are filled with surfing, and our nights are filled with sex fit for a porn film! These evening hours are filled with raucous four-play and heavenly fucking. I would sometimes pull back from this crowd of feminine excitement just to take in such a magnificent view. These are lovely images that are imbedded in my mind forever!

I think one of our neighbors is falling in love with my Argentine companion. Her partner feels and fears this also, and early one morning they clean their campsite, load their truck, and come over to say goodbye. The one woman with the growing affection for my companion, has tears in her eyes as we all wave *adios*. And then, they're gone.

My girlfriend and I don't make love for a couple of days. Maybe it's just the recovery from so much hardcore sex, but we don't have any desire.

A few days later, on one lazy afternoon, we take a long walk down the beach. We enjoy the cool afternoon breeze. After looking out toward the sea, and enjoying the serenity, we turn to each other, and kiss. And, oh man, it's a rich, deep kiss! This kiss turns into another, then another, and soon, we undress each other, and make love right there upon the sand. We share the most passionate sex possible. It's an absolute thrill for she and I to have this connection.

After our intimate expression of love, we walk into the ocean and wash off. Dripping wet, and hand in hand, we stroll back up the beach to our camp.

SORCERY

the lake of your love appears luminous
its surface is a tranquil mirror of watercolors
graceful, gentle ripples wave a friendly hello
leaves in the shallows adorn in delicate design on your skin
morning reflections tenderly grace the garden of your essence

in the quiet of the night
    the very quiet
in the soft stillness of the nocturnal
you are here, my treasure
you lie in the bliss of slumber
your breath relaxed
eyes of blue, lost in a dream
sleep now my love
we will reach out to one another at the dawning of a new day

the seduction of my heart, and this wild exploration of all that you are
I must consume the creamy bliss of your body
savor your skin
    soft as silk
travel legs of forever
kiss
    perfectly
        painted
            pink toes

my lover
my sweet lady
your alluring magic
your sorcery
    has me deep in the rapture of this ecstasy!

Homesick?

This morning I woke up thinking about how nice it would be to be back in California. Somewhere in the hours predawn, home beckoned.

If this had been a restless night back in California, I'd have taken a hot bath. That's my remedy for sleeplessness…A hot, soothing bath. Let the thoughts drift away, and soak in the warmth. The candle burns. The silence, the stillness, and the serenity of the moment…

This is one of those mornings…and my mind is wanders afar. That's alright.

My life in California…swimming at the college pool, business deals, hawks…

HAWK TOTEM

In my book, "Romance on the High Seas," I wrote about a spiritual occurence in self discovery by finding a hawk to be the 'Guide' that appears in my animal totem. It was a wonderful experience that occurred during a ceremony with a Native American medicine woman. She offered ceremony to a group of twenty of us. I was one of the beneficial recipients, and had an amazing encounter. Many people in our group didn't have the type of vision that I saw, and felt. For me, it was a tremendous illuminating journey.

Today, I am driving into town to meet with bank representatives. We are finalizing the last few steps in my purchasing a home. Because there have been many final touches on the investment, this is the fourth day in row of driving this route to town. There have been dozens of papers presented and signed.

It's a buyers market, and not owning any property for a number of years, I guess I'm a buyer. It has been a busy time for me with looking for the right place, and seeing if there's anything available in my price range. I've been inspecting many homes and trying to make a wise decision. There were a few times that I thought that this transaction was not reasonable enough for me...but here I am, driving towards town to sign the paperwork and become a home owner. In some odd way, one that I can't really calculate, I am going to borrow a huge amount of money from my bank, and make an "investment in my future"! At least that is what some folks are saying. It will feel good to finalize this business venture, all this paperwork and haggling isn't attune to my easy-going nature.

It is really a gorgeous day. It's a bright spring morning with a full blue sky! And, wispy white clouds! A typical day for this valley I am driving.

My drive from the coast to the main town is only twenty miles, so it's never a burden. I travel to town often for buying groceries and possible dinner with friends. I also use the university pool on a regular basis. (Alumni privilege).

And, it's always nice when town tasks are complete, and I'm driving out of town, toward the cozy rental on the coast.

So, here I am cruising down the highway, and right in front of my car, a large hawk swoops past! The bird's flight is perpendicular to the road, so I get a clear view of the hawk, and his impressive white and tan markings. In the hawk's talons he's holding a small creature. Perhaps a squirrel or gopher?

The hawk's flight was so unexpected, I hardly got a glimpse of what he was carrying, but I did see his prey's legs fluttering. Poor fella! He was still alive and heading for a critter heaven. I think, "good day for the hawk, bad day for the critter"! That's the way of the world, survival of the fittest!

+++

At the bank, one thing leads to another, and after two hours, we seem to be going nowhere. I thought I was just signing my life away at this meeting, and I'd be back on the coast to get some waves by early afternoon.

Eventually, the bank's representative explains to me that there are a few loopholes that need to be fixed, and everybody is working with me to finalize the transaction. After some more time and discussion, I am told that I now need a cosigner for the sale to manifest.

What! I thought you said I qualified for the loan? Well word has 'come down' that although there's no problem with the price settled on, or my down payment, there is a question of collateral. I had presented everything to the bank representatives about my book sales a month ago. They seem to know everything about my financial state, better than I do! So, what's up?

To my surprise, I didn't realize that I had left my cell phone on, and its ringing takes me out of the *arena* for a minute. The call is from a friend at the beach, and he's wondering what is going on. I start to rattle off my current situation, and he interrupts me, saying that the surf is "going off"! The winds have turned offshore, the swell is up, and the tides are perfect for a ripe surf session! All I say, "Unreal, be there in twenty minutes", and hang up.

I look at the others at the meeting and start to mutter an excuse about how getting home...important business is pressing. They look at me like, isn't this important enough?

So, we leave everything standing till tomorrow, or whenever the new necessary cosigner paperwork will be ready. This could take some time with my cosigner's (whomever that may be?) background check. Everything, of course, needs bank approval. I shake hands and walk out the door.

The drive home is even better than the drive into town! Moments earlier, and I was ready to be involved in a major investment, and I'd have been sticking my neck out there financially. I'm not a rich man, and maybe the stars, the Gods, and my friend the hawk, are all telling me to wait about making any important decision! Maybe, the Universe is saying, "Don't do this deal Lorenzo"!

I'm not asking anybody to cosign for the home. Then I'll have another party involved, and who knows how that'd turn out? I don't want to be in debt to family, or to a friend. And, do I really want to owe the bank an enormous amount of money, and make large monthly payments for years? I wouldn't own the house, the bank would! I would just be renting in the way of a mortgage payment each month to the bank!

All this, and the waves are going off at home. The surf pulled me back into a reality that I am comfortable with! Right now, surfing is exactly what I want to do, and in the waves is where I belong! My religion has saved me again!

Wow, I feel pumped! If the deal were supposed to unfold, I'd be a homeowner right now. As it is, I am relieved, revitalized, and I have a whole wad of cash that's not getting spent. Heck, I could take one tenth of that money and go on a surf sojourn for two months and I'd still be rolling in the dough!

+++

I'm driving right where I saw the hawk on my way into town. I doubt that I will see him again…and there he is, he's flying alongside the car! Oh, he's soaring so gracefully! There's no effort in his flight. He is gallant and graceful, strong and fierce. What a magnificent sight to behold! His talons have cast off any prey, and they are tucked up under his proud chest. He looks satisfied and free. Me too!

A Poem to Be Read Twenty Years from Today

I love being a poet and storyteller. Four stanzas or four pages, there are tales to be told!

From an early age, I composed verse, and stories. And then, a few of years ago, it just happened! In the middle of the night, I turned on the lamp, found paper and pen, and 'words' started pouring out of me.

The feelings behind my words came from someplace deep from within my core! The emotions came flooding out! I had no control! I had to write!

Perhaps, years from today, a surfer (young or old, active or not) will enjoy a story I wrote about sharing waves with a friend. They will read, and reflect on all the joy that surfing brings! Maybe, they'll daydream about the old times, or maybe, they'll make plans to hit the beach as soon as possible. Perhaps, arrange a summer vacation for the family at a beach, and teach the kids how to surf?

And maybe, my children will read one of my poems about love of family, and reflect on their Dad.

And years from today, late at night, a couple of lovers will read the words of a poem I wrote twenty years prior, and those words will touch something deep in their souls.

I can see the woman now…she'll have a sly smile on her face as her lover recites a sensual poem to her by candlelight. And all will be sexy and sacred.

A SLY GRIN

I am so vulnerable to a woman who has that all empowering chemistry of sensuality. Her essence revealed, and I am so open to her sexy ways! My desire to be part of her world engulfs my senses! Such intrigue! This grand allure within the universe, the wonderful energy of submerging all reason for a beautiful woman…

we are so very close
    almost touching
your scent is so inspiring
as I shut my eyes, I imagine a rich rose, and savoring its fragrance
I whisper, "Your scent, that's perfect"
    a sly grin appears on your face
I take another deep 'taste' of your thrilling aroma
you look straight at me
    almost through me
your smile hasn't disappeared
you like hearing that you make me feel so good
your sensuality is your ally

attractive you
this is my invitation to enchantment
    your hand
        your heart
you are now unforgettable

our discovery
our new world
stardust magic
hearts a fire
soul sharing
color of new, blossoms
    our beginning

THE RUNNER

I often pass the quarter mile track of the local college that the university's running team uses for working out. I have recognized some of the women runners by their unique stride and elegant posture while they circle the track. It is quite a sight to see such women in the heat of their workout. I feel that I am witnessing an elegant ballet performance. The difference between dance and sprinting is that these women runners just seem so pure, and so savage! It is the Zen of the movement.

Each of these women is beautiful in her own way, but one woman stands out more than the others. She is beautiful, and haunting. Her dark skin is fascinating, and her long legs carry her along as if she glides on air.

Today, I spot her on the other side of the field. She is pushing herself nicely around the quarter mile. We both give a wave of our hands as she completes her finish line sprint. She then walks around with her hands on her hips, trying to regain her breath. She is not too far away, so I stop at the low fence and look at her. With a glance in my direction, and in between deep breathing, she senses that I want to talk to her. She walks over.

Within a few seconds, I decide that she is radiant! She looked great from a distance, but standing a couple of feet away from her, I see she is truly magnificent! I start the conversation by mentioning that I enjoy seeing her run. She is a little embarrassed, but I think she likes hearing the compliment. I could go on about some other thoughts that are spinning around in my head; like her lips, those eyes and every sweet angle of her face, that tight stomach, the perspiration that is dripping down her absolutely hot body, and her perfect derriere; but I don't say anything, why spill the beans in the first five minutes!

We chat for a few more moments, and she tells me that she has a big race tomorrow. I end up inviting myself to watch, which seems like a good idea to her. We say goodbye and walk in opposite directions. I have to turn around a couple of times to watch her walk away. What a sight! I have no excuse for this comment about observing her wonderful sway except that it is the man within me that enjoys such a beautiful vision. All I can do is smile, and say, "thank goodness"!

THE RACE

The following morning, the field is buzzing with activities and excitement. A couple of hundred athletes are stretching and warming up. You can feel the energy of each participant as they visualize their pace on the track. The atmosphere bustles with great enthusiasm!

It takes me a few minutes to finally spot my new acquaintance, but I easily recognize this woman. She is now wearing a stretchy body suit of Lycra that has two pieces, a sports bra and shorts that actually enhance an already perfect body. I am pleased she acknowledges me with a smile. I don't want to break her focus and concentration before her race, so I don't try and get her attention. I understand that yesterday's short introduction doesn't mean we are great friends. I stay busy watching the day's events.

I finally see her as she walks toward her starting position on the track. The other women runners in her race are getting set along side of her. Her event is the 400-meter run. It is one fast lap around the track, and it's an amazing push of power and grace. The race dictates the speed these six women will carry themselves around the track, but it is considered a sprint.

I can feel the pre-race tension in the air. Each woman is so throughly focussed!

Eventually, the runners are ready, and are positioned for the race to start. In the last seconds, each woman is "one-hundred percent" for what is necessary to make a race, a race. They're about to set their bodies and minds free with an explosion of pure, highly combustible drive.

My new friend looks ready to run! I decide there is no way this woman will have a bad race. She may or may not win, but her performance will be a respectful, thrilling, and fierce!

The starting-gun *fires,* and all the women spring from their starting positions, and move into a poetic angle of thrust! Each one is Nike, the winged Goddess of Victory!

It's amazing how fast they seem to be moving! This looks like the speed of a 100-meter dash, but it is four times longer till each runner passes the finish line!

About two hundred meters into the race, and my friend is running in third position. Each runner in the event is pushing and pushing! It is a tight pack of hungry sprinters that run in unison.

By the last turn of the race, the woman in front has pushed herself too hard. Now, all the runners make their move for the lead!

My lady friend is running in second position, drafting off the frontrunner. And now, the woman, off her right shoulder, tries to blast ahead of the pack.

The last eighty meters, and it's a race between this other determined woman and my new friend. Twenty meters from the finish line, and my 'beauty', with the ravishing dark skin. The great sensuality, goes into that deep part of her core, and puts on the *after burners!* She finishes the race a full body length in front of anybody!

Did I say sensuality? I'm very happy for her and her achievement. I have to know this woman!

GODDESS OF VICTORY!

your stunning skin of brown

the graceful poetry in your rhythm

your perfection as you prance within my world

like a wild animal you explode with raw power!

I easily surrender to the gaze of your dark, dark eyes

   they are lyrics to an untamed song

I am so attracted to your wild spirit

I could watch you run all day

  I could run after you

    we could run together, side by side

let's get worn out and collapse into each other's arms

Goddess

my daylight is charmed by your movement

my night is a golden wanderlust of your essence

I delight in the mystifying way you hypnotize

I am conquered!

  You are victorious!

    All is triumphant!

NATURE OF THE BEAST, NATURE OF THE FEAST

A new day is dawning, and I'm listening to the sounds of the morning. It amazes me how we creatures stir with the sun. I am alone in bed. That's alone, not lonely! The sounds of the day are graciously singing some beautiful melodies this morning. It's the nature of the beast, or the nature of the feast.

+++

Years ago, when I taught school, I used to take the students out on the school grounds and ask them to listen carefully to everything the universe was saying. The children would be very quiet, and each would try to distinguish all the sounds of the world. Eventually, the class would have a chance to talk about what they heard. It was interesting to hear how one student might pick up a specific sound, and another student would distinguish something totally different. The sounds included so many things; cars, trucks, dogs barking, doors slamming, students on the other side of campus, the breathing of a student right next to you, the sound of someone's stuffy nose. And, back in the classroom, this would become a writing assignment, and the students would write about the experience.

Besides this exercise being fun and educational, it's also a good way to get out of the classroom and into the fresh air. Children need to experience life! They need to see and hear, taste and touch. They need to let their senses explore what is going on around them. Bookwork can be the closing door for some children's education. Don't get me wrong, books are necessary and a big part of the daily schedule, but get the students outside, let them express their inner genius in more ways than a weekly exam.

+++

It rained last night. A good storm moved through. If it were the rainy season, the precipitation probably would have lasted a few days. We probably received four inches of moisture last night.

This morning I can hear birds playing in some puddles. They're squabbling and grabbing some tasty critters for their nests. The wind has a soft, alluring whisper. The palms are gently rolling with the breeze. I can faintly catch the sound of the waves breaking on the nearby shore. In the distance, I can hear chickens and roosters. Roosters are not my favorite birds on earth. Their egos get in the way of anything constructive.

Years ago, when camping in Baja, my friend and I would leave our tent surroundings for a night, and head to the local town. We would check into book our our seperate rooms at a small lodge. The place gave us an opportunity to take a long cold shower, and wash a week's worth of sand off. Ah, a shower, and the comfort of a real bed! It sounds like a good idea. Not a good idea.

The bar up the street kept the local men going for hours. The jukebox played excessive loud music. And, around midnight, the men (being totally drunk) would head into the street and shoot their revolvers off. That's the truth. Gunshots, in the middle of the night!

The men would eventually stumble home. That's when I'd finally fall asleep. Within a few hours (about an hour before sunrise) one lone rooster would start its dawn routine of *sounding-off*. Soon, dozens of the town's roosters would do their best to show which one had the biggest *cajones*. Jeez, it was Dante's Inferno! After that one experience, we passed on spending nights at the lodge.

Throughout the years, I've gone from using a sleeping bag on the beach, to staying at some comfy, first class resorts. It's all about one's comfort zone.

I love camping, and still do. There's simplicity in a lone campfire. Folks may wander over to the fireside for some conversation. We'd play guitars and hand drums. Maybe tell a joke or two. These jokes would include sex, blondes, golf, and of course, attorneys. Ah, lawyers, always the brunt of a good joke.

If I'd studied law, and had become an attorney, I'd have specialized in art and antiquities. Treasure hunters, rich companies and foreign countries would have wanted my expertise pertaining to lost treasure, and who rightfully owns it. As a world famous lawyer, I would have been sent to study archives in Spain so to unravel an newly discovered *treasure chest. The bounty*, worth millions.

My young assistant would be an exquisite Spanish beauty. Her thick dark hair would fall over 16th Century documents we studied. Eventually, and somewhere toward midnight, she and I would come together in a romantic frenzy. This is after we had deciphered the secret answer to our studies, and the multi-million dollar treasure. Wrapped in each other's arms, we would have to make mad, spectacular love atop of four-hundred-year-old maps and legal papers!

I should write all this down, it has imagination...

I can hear the breaking waves in the distance. I better stroll down to check the surf.

This is a good place to end this chapter, but...

There's comfort in picking up my surfboard, having it rest securely under my arm. I'm filled with wonder and anticipation for the surf that will soon be ridden. I love the salt water baptismal, and taking that first wave. The first time, or the ten-thousandth time, it feels correct. It's always high adventure! This feeling of satisfaction is the same feeling a seasoned fisherman knows with his trusty, prize rod in his hands, or how a satisfied housewife feels when cooking on her own kitchen stove. Or how an over zealous sports fan feels with the TV remote control firmly in their grip. Everybody has their comfort zone.

This is a good place to end this chapter, but...

If I don't write a few of these colorful ideas down before I get back from surfing, I'll forget 90% of everything that I've been daydreaming!

OK, let's see...

bed and alone
morning and sounds
school and the students
nature studies and roosters
Baja and campfires
jokes and lawyers
buried treasure and Spanish beauty
millions of dollars and spectacular sex
surfboard and that first step onto the sand

THE RISING SUN

May morning of miracles
my senses are flattered
    they hold every awareness

gentle wind through the Sycamore
    sings of rustling leaves
aroma of the orange blossoms
    enters
        through an elegant sunrise

so beautiful
    the lone canoe
        on a windless lake

yawning sky
    rich sapphire blue
        imaginary faces on those snowy clouds

protected from all earth questions
  I can find no reason to ask or examine

sweet mystical music of the universe

BABIES, ANGELS FROM HEAVEN

I discovered a small medical facility in town. A doctor from a neighboring village comes to the clinic once a week to help the local families with whatever medical needs are necessary. There's also a full-time nurse that treats the locals with knowledge and kindness. I've been volunteering once a week. No specific day, so sometimes the doctor is around, and sometimes it's just the nurse.

I organize and stock shelves, clean and disinfect, and occasionally assist with young children still while the doctor is stitching them up. It feels good to 'lend a hand'. The staff and community appreciate my help.

Over the years, I've been fortunate enough to pull a couple of helpless people out of the surf when they were in trouble. Assisting these people was necessary, and apparently the Universe wanted me to be the one to pull the out of the water. So, who knows what the psychological theory is behind my volunteering at the medical facility. Who knows and who cares? I believe that a little hands-on grass roots assistance can only benefit the world. And, perhaps helping those less fortunate strokes my own ego. Hey, if it inspires and nutures my life, I accept and honor it.

This last week the doctor was not around when a pregnant woman came into the clinic. She showed up with her other two children; one in her arms, and the other hanging onto her skirt. She was in labor and the birth of her next child would be within the hour.

The nurse started giving me orders, and luckily she speaks enough English for me to understand. I was hoping other local women would have been around the clinic to help with midwifery, and the woman's labor...but for some odd reason, the medical center was void of any patients that afternoon. Luckily, a woman was walking on the street outside the clinic, and heard the mother moaning. This woman assisted in watching the two children as we began the birthing procedures.

The birth of her new baby boy brought tears to my eyes and a huge smile to my face. I couldn't get rid of that smile for hours. All went well in delivery and I felt blessed to be part of the sacred ceremony. This experience brought me closer to the mother, the nurse, and the folks in the community.

What a world of women and men, and the bringing forth of children! I reflect back on the birth of my own two children. I can honestly say, that those two births are the greatest experiences of my life! I cherish being a father! And, I am sure I share this sentiment with most parents.

After my experience with the baby's birth at the clinic, word spread around town and among the local moms and dads. Apparently, I'm quite knowledgeable within the medical profession. Ha, Ha! All I did was hold the mother's hand, and bestowed encouragement. The mom, and the nurse, did all the work. I'm not foolish though, I'll take all the good public relations I can get. The local community opened their hearts, and welcomed me like never before.

At the beach, other day, some kids started calling me "El Doctor"!

Young at Heart

This peninsula has its locals and it has its visitors. I have made friends with both groups, and I have also steered clear of a few folks. One expatriate that has lived around here for years is spmeone I'd rather not run into on the street. At first, I tried and be friendly, and show that *aloha* spirit. But, because he won't look on the bright side of things, I now avoid him. He always complains about what's wrong with America. He swings any conversation to politics and Hollywood gossip.

OK, I get it, but I don't want to talk about that. I don't want to debate you buddy! Or, listen to your rants and raves. You have a few good points, but get out of my face! Didn't you leave America to get away from the politics and television gossip?

I finally told him just that, and it worked...now, he simply acknowleges me, and keeps on walking.

Some college kids, a young man boy and woman, from Vancouver Island have been around for a couple of weeks. They are learning to surf. I've enjoyed their company very much. We've shared a few dinners. And at the beach, I've instructed them on how to catch a wave and how to read what is going on in the ocean. They've been polite and appreciative. More people in the world should be like these two. And, I should visit Vancouver Island. There's another arrow on my map.

There are local children that use their beach for every type of game invented. Boys and girls are included in this gathering of friends. On lazy afternoons, the kids get into running in and out the sea, battling it out with laughter and wrestling.

I think back to when my brother and I used to wrestle, in just the same way. Seven and ten-year-olds know how to use their time wisely! Never a dull moment! We'd compete, encourage, hang out, ride our bikes, stay up late, climb trees, play army, play tackle football, share ice-cold drinks, and get into some *not-so-terrible-trouble.*

My brother and I used to make believe we were having a fistfight. The local pool would be a good place for this high drama, Shakespearean acting. We would swing and miss the face by a few inches, and clap our hands as to make our audience think that a fist cleanly hit our jaw. And then we'd fall into the water. God, we were good! We fooled everybody. It wasn't till I was a grown man that I realized that the adults were playing along with our charade.

It is good to be young in mind and spirit. Maybe that is what many of us are trying to accomplish in life, to stay young at heart? Maybe this is why I surf, and why I adore and dream women? I don't feel old at all!

I know what you are thinking; a psychoanalyst could have a field day with me. Hey, I don't care what you think…it's a good life, so I live it with passion, grace and confidence!

A Conversation with Drums

My brother and I had a couple of sets of bongo drums when we were kids. Many nights, we would sit together, and 'talk' with the drums. Our drum conversations were filled with rhythm; the rhythm of the earth, family, youth, emotions, laughter. It was our chatting about the world.

He, and then I, would trade off playing some expressionistic riff on the bongos. Each would interpret what we were feeling through the drum. It worked exceptionally well.

Sometimes the drumming would just move on in its own direction. Although it was just the two of us, I guess this was our introduction to a drum circle.

This was always fun, and we'd have a big smile across our faces while drumming. This was our secret, ancient means of communication. It was our expression, or language, of our universe. A voice spoken between brothers.

I Can't Stop Myself!

my first glimpse, so many years ago, on the campus of UC Berkeley
there were these drummers, and they had this delicious, smiling spirit
the sound they were making, it was trance-like
and women were dancing
beautiful women
wonderful images that still lovingly haunt my memory
my spell had been cast

it's the sound of the drums, the dancers moving
feel it?
it's the rhythm, and it's intoxicating!
this is one of life's grand occasions
this is a ceremony to set oneself free!

it's an infectious beating of drums, shakers and bells
the origin is from ancient Africa, and the scattered islands of the Caribbean
it's primitive, holy, rich and it's flaming!

tonight, I am sharing in a celebration
we're all dancing along to a contagious, driving beat
we are all moving, just in the moment, and we're released from boundaries
wardrobe or hair, no one cares
there's no past, no future
just the now
dancing to the infectious rhythm of life
this is a tribe
a tribe of wild souls
we have all cheerfully gathered to share in a basic ritual
the ritual of celebrating the earth's heartbeat

my heart is happy, and I can't stop myself!

I can't stop myself!

In Search Of Happiness

I don't have any excuse for the life I have chosen, it's clear, simple and relevant. Months ago, I made changes within my life, and moved my world to include this quiet coastline. Now, I rejoice in the vitality of the *present*. And, there will be a day when I'll return to California. And, when that day arrives, I'll embrace that reality with a smile.

I've been reflecting on what the universe is providing in my life. It's full with memorable adventures, valuable lessons and clarifying revelations. My greatest gift is that I've been blessed with two of amazing children. Their souls lit a burning love in me that cannot be extinguished!

Like others, I've struggled with my share of tough times, but my spirit has always stayed positive. I keep a smile on my face, and in my heart. It's the Zen of it all.

Today, I have been scouting the beach for more shells. Not sure what I will do with the all these shells I have been collecting when the time to leave this coast. I imagine I'll keep a few and save a few for gifts, and return the rest to where they came from, our mother ocean.

ARCHER

mystifying feathers shine
the arrow's swift release
    whisper of silent strength

firmly, I grip the bow
it is as if the ancients have entered my soul
    clarity of a past vision
heart centuries of survival
      the myth
      the hunt
      the protection of the tribes
my perception of bow and archer becoming one

exotic woods
    respected workmanship
Maple, Birch, Rosewood, Zebra
    Vermont, Honduras, Africa

keen, concentrated motion of hands and arms
    eyes of confidence
all is a metaphor
    a revelation
an incentive to express simplicity
    accuracy
        proficiency

mystifying feathers shine
the arrow's swift release

VILLA DULCE

through my window
    the sea
I feel the morning glimpse of angels shouting
    laughter from the heavens
this divine road of experience
it all gathers
    and grabs me!
        shakes me!
wild and uninhibited!

I climb toward a collected aura, and I applaud it all
behold a grand orchestra of color and hope
there is the kiss of brilliance
    that tickles the breeze of a sacred spirit
this presence moves
    through this house
        through my life
such a soothing seduction

these are winds of change
    winds of a dream
this is the structure of my world
I found that the journey is my mentor
    my metaphor for this life

this gradual intertwining of souls and the cosmos
this zenith daylight within!
    the lavish night within!
I laugh at an unlimited sky
oh, gentle flood of stars and light
water iridescent
our fire earth
this harvest of bliss
it all sticks to my skin
    and slowly seeps within

my sight is clear
my heart open
    my heart mixes with all hearts
all my aspirations
all my amazement
all is pure, unique, and full with eloquence
my spirit expands

HOMEWARD BOUND

I find that I have been standing in my front yard most every night for an hour or so. There is a spiritual connection to stand here and look up into the nighttime sky. I write verse before and after, but I am not thinking about poems or stories when I am in this sacred spot.

I have no clock, but it must be between 10 p.m. and midnight. The growing moon has appeared in one corner of the sky, and I track its movement from time to time. It should be full in about a week. Stars shine brightly on this lost coast. There are no lights from towns or cars, so I get an unobstructed view of the celestial treats that pulsate throughout the heavens. I wonder if the powerful ones that form as star clusters are having any influence over my destiny. I look forward to this silent chat with myself and with the Universe every night.

In these last few months, I've awakened some new aspirations in my life. I better understand what I must focus on in my future, and in my present. It was so necessary for me to leave the safety and security of my home in the States, and see what new adventure was just waiting to be unearthed. Here, on this tropic coast, I have established some new, lasting friendships. It was also a pleasant surprise to have some friends from California visit. They appreciated the warmth of the ocean and the warmth we all share as friends. I have lots of acquaintances, but only a few people I can call *true friends*. With a winter filled with grand and gracious waves to grand and gracious women, the blessings have been plentiful!

This has been an exceptional place to live for this winter and most of the spring. Although I haven't thought about missing anything special back home, I think I am ready to leave this cottage and the café, this beach and these warm waves, this jungle and this quiet coast. Perhaps this spark to go home is because next month I will visit Europe. I am looking forward to my rendezvous with the special lady in Italy. Time may have diminished the elevated and ambitious expectations of love, but there is only one way to find out, so it will be good to see what happens next with "love."

Traveling is a great excuse to grow. If we look at each sojourn as a lesson in life our travels are full of growth. I look forward to my departure from home, living the experience and then returning home. I appreciate where I come from, and homeward bound has just as much wonder and awe as the escape. It is all part of the eternal journey.

I know in my future that I will dream about distant waves and warm tropic nights. After the chores and work are done, maybe I will find someplace on a map that I have been thinking about visiting. Perhaps I will hear of an island that has amazing surf, pure white beaches and exotic women with such beauty that it should all be rhythmically composed into poetry.

Let the adventures begin and let them blossom.